The Penniless Lords

In want of a wealthy wife

Meet Daniel, Gabriel, Lucien and Francis.
Four lords, each down on his fortune and
each in need of a wife of means.

From such beginnings, can these marriages of
convenience turn into something
more treasured than money?

Don't miss this enthralling new quartet by
Sophia James

Read Daniel, Gabriel, Lucien
and Francis's stories in

Marriage Made in Money

Marriage Made in Shame

Marriage Made in Rebellion

Marriage Made in Hope

All available now!

D0756537

4721800019197 6

Author Note

I've loved writing The Penniless Lords series. Each of the four lords has his own particular set of problems, and Francis St Cartmail, the damaged Earl of Douglas, is no exception.

Hounded by his past, and lonely with it, Francis finds his world turned around when he saves a woman from drowning in the Thames.

Lady Sephora Connaught is suffocating in life even before she falls into the river, and when a stranger pulls her from certain death it's as if she has crossed a threshold and everything has changed.

Christine, who is Lucien's sister, is next. I have written her story as a novella for a forthcoming Christmas anthology.

MARRIAGE MADE IN HOPE

Sophia James

MILLS & BOON

All rights reserved including the right of reproduction in whole
or in part in any form. This edition is published by arrangement with
Harlequin Books S.A.

This is a work of fiction. Names, characters, places, locations and
incidents are purely fictional and bear no relationship to any real
life individuals, living or dead, or to any actual places, business
establishments, locations, events or incidents. Any resemblance is
entirely coincidental.

This book is sold subject to the condition that it shall not, by way of
trade or otherwise, be lent, resold, hired out or otherwise circulated
without the prior consent of the publisher in any form of binding or
cover other than that in which it is published and without a similar
condition including this condition being imposed on the subsequent
purchaser.

® and TM are trademarks owned and used by the trademark owner
and/or its licensee. Trademarks marked with ® are registered with the
United Kingdom Patent Office and/or the Office for Harmonisation in
the Internal Market and in other countries.

Published in Great Britain 2016
by Mills & Boon, an imprint of HarperCollins*Publishers*
1 London Bridge Street, London, SE1 9GF

© 2016 Sophia James

ISBN: 978-0-263-91704-8

Our policy is to use papers that are natural, renewable and
recyclable products and made from wood grown in sustainable
forests. The logging and manufacturing processes conform to the
legal environmental regulations of the country of origin.

Printed and bound in Spain
by CPI, Barcelona

Sophia James lives in Chelsea Bay, on Auckland, New Zealand's North Shore, with her husband, who is an artist. She has a degree in English and History from Auckland University and believes her love of writing was formed by reading Georgette Heyer in the holidays at her grandmother's house. Sophia enjoys getting feedback at sophiajames.co

Books by Sophia James

Mills & Boon Historical Romance

The Penniless Lords

Marriage Made in Money
Marriage Made in Shame
Marriage Made in Rebellion
Marriage Made in Hope

Men of Danger

Mistletoe Magic
Mistress at Midnight
Scars of Betrayal

The Wellingham Brothers

High Seas to High Society
One Unashamed Night
One Illicit Night
The Dissolute Duke

Stand-Alone Novels

Knight of Grace
Lady with the Devil's Scar
Gift-Wrapped Governesses
'Christmas at Blackhaven Castle'

Visit the Author Profile page
at millsandboon.co.uk for more titles.

Chapter One

London—1815

Lady Sephora Connaught knew that she was going to die. Right then and there as the big black horse bucked on the bridge and simply threw her over the balustrade and down into the fast-running river.

Her sister screamed and so did others, the sounds blocked out by the water as she hit it, fright taking breath and leaving terror. She exhaled from pure instinct, but still the river came in, filling her mouth and throat and lungs as the cloth of her heavy skirt drew her under to the darkness and the gloom. She could not fight it, could not gain purchase or traction or leverage.

Ripping at her riding jacket, she tried to loosen the fastenings, but it was hopeless. There were too many buttons and beneath that too many stays, too much boning and layers and tightness, all clinging and covering and con-stricting.

This was it.

The moment of her end; already the numb-ness was coming, the pain in her leg from hit-ting the balustrade receding into acceptance, the light from above fading as she sank amongst the fish and the mud and the empty blackness. It was over. Her life. Her time. Gone before she had even lived it. Her hands closed over her mouth and nose so that she would not breathe in, but her lungs were screaming for air and she couldn't deny them further.

A movement above had her tipping her head, the disturbance of the water felt more than seen as a dark shape came towards her. A man fully dressed, his hand reaching out even as he kicked. She simply watched, trying to deter-mine if he could be real, here in the depths of the Thames, here where the light was failing and all warmth was gone.

God, the girl had simply given up, floating there like a giant jellyfish, skirts billowing, hair streaming upwards, skin pale as moonlight and eyes wide.

Why did the gentlemen of the *ton* not teach their daughters to swim, for heaven's sake? If they had, she might have made a fist of her own salvation and tried to strike out for the surface. Anything but this dreadful final acceptance and lack of fight. His mouth came tight across her own as he gave her breath, there in the dark and cold, the last of his air before he kicked upwards, fingers anchored around her arm. At least she did not struggle, but came with him like a sodden dead weight, the emerald hue of a riding jacket the only vivid.thing about her.

And then they were up into the sun and the wind and the living, bouncing like corks in the quick-cut current of the river, her legs wound about his like a vice, one hand scratching down the side of his face and drawing blood as she tried to grab him further.

'Damn it. Keep still.' His words were rasped out through shattered breath and lost in open space.

But she would not calm, the flailing panic pulling him under, her eyes wide with terror. Swearing again, he jammed her hard in against

him and made for the bank whilst keeping with
the current, glad when he saw others running
down the pathways to reach them in the mire
of sludge and slurry.

The mud from Hutton's Landing came back
in memory, falling across him, pulling him
down, thick as molasses, heavy as oil, and he
began to shiver. Violently. It was everywhere
here, too, around his legs, across the stockings
on his feet, staining the full skirts of the girl,
her body pinned to his own like a well-fitting
glove and taking any last remaining warmth.

He needed to be gone, to be home, away
from the prying eyes of others and the pity he
so definitely did not want. She was retching now
violently, water streaming from her mouth as
oxygen took the place of the putrid contents of
the Thames. She was shaking, too. Shock, he
supposed, feeling his own gathering panic. He
was glad when a stranger reached out to lift her
from him as Gabriel Hughes and Lucien Howard joined him on the bank.

Others were there also, an older woman
screaming and a younger girl telling her to be
quiet. Men as well, their eyes sharply observing

him as he lumbered out, the old scar no doubt in full blaze across his face.

He could not hide anything. The shaking. The anger. The hatred. He was caught only in limbo, in memory and in mud.

'Come, Francis. We will take you home.'

Gabriel's voice came through the fury, his hand slipping around the sodden sleeve of his friend's coat as he led him off. The girl was crying now, but Francis did not look back. Not even once.

She couldn't stop the sobbing or quell her fear, even as those around her shouted out orders to fetch a carriage, to find some blankets, to get a doctor and to staunch the flow of blood on her right shin.

She was alive and breathing. She was sitting on the solidness of soil and earth, perched in the thin sun of a late spring afternoon on a pathway near the Thames with all the life she thought she had lost now back in front of her.

'We will get you home, Sephora, right now. Richard has gone to find a carriage and a runner has been sent to make certain your father is informed of what has happened here.'

Her mother's voice sounded odd, strained by worry, probably, and abject fright.

Sephora closed her eyes and tried to push things back and away. She could barely contemplate what had happened and she felt removed somehow, from the people, from the river bank, even from the earth upon which she sat.

Shock, perhaps? Or some other malady that came from swallowing too much water? The horror of it all swirled in, taking away the colour of the day, and her skin felt clammy and odd. Then all she knew was darkness.

She woke during the night in the Aldford town house on Portman Square, the candle next to her bed throwing shadows across the ceiling and a fire blazing in the hearth.

Maria, her sister, sat close on a chair, eyes closed and a shawl pushed away from her nightgown because of the warmth. Asleep. Sephora smiled and stretched. She felt better, more herself. She felt warm and safe and whole. There was a bandage around the bottom of her right leg and it hurt to push against it, but apart from that… She did a quick inventory of her body and found everything else in good working order and painless.

The memory of a mouth across hers in the water came back like a punch to the stomach. Her saviour had given her air when she was without it, ten feet under in the dark, the last of his own store and precious. Her heart began to race violently and she turned, her sister coming awake at the small movement, eyes focusing as she leaned forward.

'You look better, Sephora.'

'How did I look before?' Her voice was raspy and stretched. A surprising sound, that, and she coughed.

'Half-dead.'

'The horse…?'

'He bolted on the bridge and bucked you off. A bee sting, the groom said afterwards, and a bad one. Father has sworn he'll sell the stallion for much less than he paid for it, too, as he wants nothing more to do with it.'

Privately Sephora was glad that she would never need to see the steed again.

'Do you remember anything of what happened?' Her sister's tone had a new note now, one of interest and speculation.

'I remember someone saved me?'

'Not just any someone either. It was the Earl of Douglas, Francis St Cartmail, the black sheep of the *ton*. It's been the talk of the town.'

'Where was Richard?'

'Right behind where you were on the bridge, frozen solid in fright. I don't think he can swim. Certainly he did not tear off his boots as the earl did and simply dive in.'

'St Cartmail did that?'

'With barely a backward glance. The water was fast flowing there and the bridge is high, but he most assuredly did not look in any way concerned as he vaulted on to the narrow balustrade.'

'And dived in?'

'Like a pirate.' Her sister began to smile. 'Like a pirate with his face slashed by a scar and his long dark hair loose and flowing down his back.'

Sephora remembered nothing of his countenance, only the touch of warm lips against her own, intimate and forbidden under the murky waters of the Thames.

'Was he hurt?'

'He was when he got out of the river because

you had scratched his face. There were three vivid lines down his other cheek and they were running with blood.'

'But someone helped him?'

'Lords Wesley and Ross. They did not stay around, though, for by the time he had got to the pathway the Earl of Douglas looked even sicker than you did.'

Francis St Cartmail, the fifth Earl of Douglas. Sephora turned the name over in her mind. So many swirling rumours about him in the *ton*, a lord who lived on the seedier side of rightness and amongst an underworld of danger.

She had only ever seen him once and at a distance in the garden of the Creightons' ball two months prior. There he had been entwined in the arms of a woman who was known for her questionable morals and loose ways, rouged lips turned to his in supplication. Miss Amelia Bourne, standing with Sephora, had been quick to relay the gossip that surrounded the earl, her eyes full of infatuation and interest.

'Douglas is beautiful, is he not, even with that scar and though he is seen less and less frequently in social company these days, when he does appear there is always gossip. I, for one, should not listen to any such slander if a man could kiss me like that…?' Amelia let the rest slide into query as she laughed.

Sephora had returned home after that particular ball and dreamed of what it must feel like to be kissed with such complete abandon, wild beauty and open lustfulness.

Well, now she almost knew in a way.

Shaking away that heated thought, she sat up. 'Is there something to drink?'

Her sister poured her a full glass of sweetened lemonade with mint and rosemary leaves on top and helped her to sip it.

'Where is Richard?'

'He was in the library last evening with Father, trying to smooth down the gossip and contain the rumour that is rife around the *ton*.'

'Rumour?' Sephora could not quite understand what was said. Gesturing to Maria that she had had enough of the lemonade, she lay back.

'You were wrapped around Douglas like a blanket from head to toe as he came to the bank and it seemed to us as if you did not wish to let go. Richard had to pry open your fingers from St Cartmail's personage.'

'I was drowning.'

'You were wanton. The front of your jacket had been ripped open and the material on your bodice was gaping.' This summary was accompanied by a hearty laugh. 'And it suited you. You looked magnificently alive.'

Sephora ignored that nonsense completely. 'Where is Mama?'

'In bed after ingesting a stiff toddy. She should be out until the morrow so you shan't have to deal with her worry. The one thing she did keep saying over and over was that at least you and Richard Allerly had announced your betrothal so you were not entirely ruined.'

'It was hardly my fault the horse reacted so violently.'

'Mama would say drowning might have been altogether more circumspect given the intimate clutch your rescuer held you in and your dreadful state of undress.'

Sephora smiled. 'You have always exaggerated events, Maria, but thank you for staying here with me at least. It is a comfort.'

Her sister took her hand in her own, the soft warmth of her grip familiar. 'You have lost Richard's diamond ring in the incident. I do not think he knows this fact yet and will probably not be well pleased.'

'It was always too big and I saw the exact pattern in Rundell's when I was in the shop a few weeks ago so it shouldn't be too difficult to replace.'

Maria laughed. 'Just like Richard to settle for a cheap stock item, Sephora, when you plainly deserve so much more.'

'I was happy with it.'

'I doubt Francis St Cartmail would be so stingy with his newfound money were he to be wed. It is said he returned from the Americas as a wealthy man made rich from the striking of gold. He looked awfully sick after your rescue, though, almost falling over in fact with…a sort of shaking panic. I hope he is recovered.'

Sephora remembered that suddenly, the bone-deep weariness of him as he had struggled the last few yards through the mud. 'Was he hurt anywhere else?'

'Apart from your scratches to his face, you mean?'

When she nodded, Maria went on.

'Not that I could see. I wondered why the earl did not stay to receive the adulation of those who had observed the rescue, though, even given his questionable reputation. It was a fine and daring thing he did and the water is deep there in the middle and cold. Richard was standing next to you, of course, with his thousand-yard stare and his implacable credentials. Perhaps that is what put Francis St Cartmail off?'

'I don't even remember Richard being there at all. I know he was on the horse beside me, I recall that, but after...'

'Douglas and his two friends were walking the other way when you screamed. They had just got to the bridge.'

Dark hair and dark clothes and the feel of knotted skin under her fingers as she had reached for him and held on.

Somehow those few moments seemed more real to Sephora than anything else in her entire life. A reaction, she supposed, to her near drowning and the fright of it, for nothing truly dreadful had ever happened to her before. Maria was watching her carefully, the beginnings of a frown across her brow.

'Do you ever think, Sephora, that incidents like this might happen for a reason?'

'A reason?'

'You have not looked happy of late and you have seemed distracted. Ever since you agreed to become Richard's bride, come to think of it. He has all the money in the world, a beautiful house and a family who think he is stellar and that is not even taking into account his position in society, but...' She stopped.

'You never liked him, Maria. Ever since the start.'

'He is pompous and self-righteous, always congratulating himself on his next achievement and his latest triumph.'

Despite herself Sephora began to laugh. 'He does a lot of good for others...'

'And more than good for himself,' her sister countered.

'He is kind to his family...'

'And kinder to those who can aid him in his steady ascent to power within the *ton*.'

'He loves me.'

Maria nodded. 'Yes, I will give him that, but who does not adore you, Sephora? I have never yet met a soul who says a bad word of you and that includes the numerous suitors you've let down gently in their quest for your hand.'

'You give me too much praise, Maria.'

Sometimes I am not nice. Sometimes I could scream with the boredom of being exactly who it is I have become. Sometimes there is another person in me just under the surface struggling for breath and freedom.

The touch of St Cartmail's lips to her mouth, the feel of his hand across her neck, firm and forceful. The whispered shared air that he'd given her when she had held no more herself.

Douglas had lifted her into his arms like a child, as though she weighed nothing, as though he might have carried her the length of the river and never felt it. There was a certain security in the strength of a man, she thought, a protection and a magic. Richard would barely be able to lift her with his city body and thinness.

Comparisons.

Why on earth was she making them? St Cartmail was wild and worrying and unknown. She had heard he had killed a man in the Americas and got away with it.

The following morning she felt as if she had been run over by a heavy piece of machinery, the muscles that had been sore yesterday now making themselves known in a throbbing ache of pain.

Her mother's quiet knock on the door had her turning. 'I am so thankful to see you looking well rested, my dear, as you gave us all a terrible fright yesterday. But it is late in the morning now and Richard is here, wondering if he might just have a quick word.'

Elizabeth sat on the chair beside the bed, the heavy frown across her brow very noticeable today. 'We could get you dressed and looking presentable while he talks with Father. It would be a good thing for you to be up and about for it pays to get back on the horse after such a fright…' She stopped, suddenly realising just what she had said. 'Not literally, of course, and certainly not that dreadful stallion. But normality must return and the sooner that it does the better.'

Sephora felt like simply rolling over and pulling the blankets up across herself, keeping everyone at bay. If she said she was not up to seeing Richard, would he go away or would he insist upon seeing her? He was not a man inclined to wait for anything and sometimes under the genial smile she could detect a harder irritation that concerned her.

She knew she could not stay here tucked away in the safety of her bedroom forever after such a difficulty and she also understood that to put their meeting off was only postponing the problem.

Pushing back the bedding, Sephora rose up into the morning and was glad when her maid came in to help her dress.

As Richard entered the small blue salon Sephora could see her mother hovering on the edges of her vision, just to make certain everything was proper and correct, that propriety was observed and manners obeyed.

'My dear.' His hands were warm when he took hers, the brown in his eyes deep today and worried. 'My dearest, dearest girl. I am so very sorry.'

'Sorry?' Sephora could not quite understand his meaning.

'I should have come after you, of course. I should not have hesitated, but I am a poor swimmer, you see, and the water there is very deep...' He stopped, as if realising that the more he said the less gallant he appeared. 'If I had lost you…?'

'Well, you did not, Richard, and truth be told I am largely unharmed and almost over it.'

'Your leg?'

'A small cut from where I hit the stone balustrade, but nothing more. I doubt there will even be a scar.'

'I sent a note to thank Douglas so that you should have no need for further discourse with him. I am just sorry it was not Wesley or Ross who rescued you, for they would have been much easier to thank.'

'In what way?' Disengaging his hands, she sat with hers in her lap. She felt suddenly cold.

'They are gentlemen. I doubt Douglas has much of a notion of the word at all. Did you see the way he just left without discourse or acknowledgement? A gentleman would have at least tarried to make certain you were alive. At that point you barely looked it.'

Sephora remembered vomiting again and again over Francis St Cartmail as they had waded in from the deep, seawater and tears mixed across the deep brown of his ruined jacket. He wore a ring, she thought, trying to recall the design and failing. It sat on the little finger of his left hand, a substantial gold-and-ruby cabochon.

'I took you from him at the water's edge, Sephora. My own riding jacket suffered, of course, but at least you were safe and sound. A groom found a blanket to put around you and I sent for my carriage and marshalled all those about us into some sort of an order. Quite a fracas, really, and a fair bit of organisation to see things in order on my part, but I am glad it has turned out so well in the end.'

Sephora mused over all the things Richard had done for her, all the help and good intentions, the carriage filled with warm woollen blankets, his solicitousness and his worry so very on show.

She began to cry quite suddenly, a feeling that welled from the bottom of her stomach and swelled into her throat, a pounding, horrible unladylike howl that tore at her heart and her sense and her modesty. Unstoppable. Inexplicable. Desperate.

Her mother rushed over and took her in warm arms and Richard left the room with as much haste as he could politely manage. Sephora was glad he was gone.

'Men never have an inkling of what to say in a time of crisis, my love. Richard was indeed wonderful with his orders and his arrangements and his wisdom. We could not have wished for more.'

'More?' Her one-worded question fell into silence.

He had not dived into the water after her, he had not risked his life for her. Instead he had simply watched her fall and sink, down and down into the greying dark coldness of the river without breath or hope.

Richard had done what he thought was enough and he was her betrothed. She had never met the Earl of Douglas and yet Francis St Cartmail had, without thought, jumped in to save her there amongst the frigid green depths.

She had no touchstone any more for what was true and what was not. Her life had been turned upside down by a single unselfish act into question and uncertainty and lost in the confusion of reality—these seconds, these moments, this morning with the sun coming in through wide windows and open sashes.

If Lord Douglas had not come to her, she would have been lying now instead on a cold marble slab in the family mausoleum, drowned by misadventure, the unlucky tragic Lady Sephora Connaught, twenty-two and a half and gone.

Her nails dug into the skin above her wrists, leaving whitened crescents that stung badly, and she liked the pain. It told her she was alive, but the numbness inside around her heart was spreading and there was nothing at all she could do to stop it.

Chapter Two

After the rescue at the river Francis removed his sodden jacket and lay down on the day bed in his library, closing his eyes against sickness. Everything upon him was wet, but just for this moment he needed to be still.

It always happened like this, suddenly, shockingly, placing him out of kilter with all that was around him and sending him back to other moments, other times, other places that he never wanted to remember.

Even the change of environment did not banish the panic, though it made the waiting easier here amongst his books and his throat stopped feeling quite so blocked and swollen.

'Have a drink, Francis. Then if you do happen to die on us you will at least have the rancid filthy taste of the Thames gone from your mouth.' Gabriel handed him a large glass of brandy filled to the rim as he sat up and took two generous sips before placing it down.

'This has…happened before. It's not…fatal. It's…just damn…unpleasant.' He was still shaking and his voice reflected it, ice in his bones and shards of glass in his head. He was so very tired.

'Why?' One word from Lucien, hard and angry. 'It's the Hutton's Landing affair, isn't it? That damn blunder with Seth Greenwood and somehow his death is your problem forever.'

Francis shook his head.

'It's the…mud.'

'The mud?'

'The mud that covered us. The memory comes back sometimes…and I can't fight off the feeling.'

'God, Francis. You went to America as one man and came back as altogether a different one. Richer, I will agree, but…altered in a way that makes you brittle and you won't let us in to help you.'

Francis tried to concentrate, to sift through all of the extraneous matter and find out what was important.

'Who was…she?'

'The girl you pulled from the Thames? You don't know?' Lucien began to smile. 'That was Lady Sephora Connaught, the uncrowned "angel of the *ton*", the woman who every other female aspires to become like…and one who is engaged to Richard Allerly.'

'The Marquis of Winslow. The duke's son?'

'His only son. The golden couple. Both sets of parents are good friends. Bride and groom-to-be have known each other since childhood and the relationship has matured into more. It will be the wedding of the year.'

Gabriel on the other side of the room was less inclined to sugar-coat it. 'Allerly is an idiot and you know it, too, Luce, as well as being a damned coward.'

For the first time in an hour Francis felt his shivering lessen with this turn of topic. 'How is he a coward?'

'Winslow was there, damn it, right behind his would-be bride. He watched as that untrained horse of hers upended her over the balustrade and sent her tumbling down into the river.'

'And he did…nothing?'

'Well, he certainly didn't take a leap from a

high bridge into a deep and fast-running river without thinking twice. Cowering against the stonework might be a better description of his reaction. The skin on his knuckles was white from the grip.'

Lucien looked as though he found Gabriel's description more than amusing. 'Allerly was there soon enough though when you got her to the bank, Francis, I noticed he tried not to get mud on his new boots as he all but snatched her from you.'

'Hardly snatched,' Gabriel countered. 'It did look as if the girl knew who her saviour was at least and it took the marquis a while to get her to let you go. Her bodice was ripped, too. Her beloved took a good long look at what was on offer beneath before taking off his own jacket to cover her. Sephora Connaught's mother, Lady Aldford, looked less than pleased with him.'

For the first time in hours Francis relaxed. 'It seems as if Lady Sephora made quite an impression on you both.'

Gabriel took up the rebuttal. 'We are happily married men, Francis. It's you we hope might have noticed her obvious charms.'

'Well, I didn't. I was shaking too much.'

He leaned back against the sofa and drew a blanket across himself before finishing the rest of the strong brandy. The name was familiar and he tried to place it.

'Lady Sephora Connaught. How is it I know of her?'

'She is Anne-Marie McDowell's youngest cousin.'

Anne-Marie. He had courted her once a good many years ago, but she had died of some quick sickness before they could take the relationship to the next stage. He'd got drunk when he'd found out, so blindingly drunk he'd never made it to her funeral. Looking back, he thought his reactions had come not so much from the shock of Anne-Marie's death but from the reminder that the grim reaper took people randomly, with no thought of age or experience or character.

The family had not been pleased by his absence though and he knew now he should have handled things with more aplomb than he had.

His right cheek ached from where Sephora Connaught had scratched him, three dark lines running from eye to chin caught in the reflection of the glass that he held. He hoped they would not fester like the wound had on the other cheek as he closed his eyes.

When he had thrown himself off the bridge today part of him had hoped he might not again surface and that he would be celebrated as a hero when he failed to reappear. Such a legacy of valour might sweeten the nightly howls of the Douglas ancestors whose portraits lined the steep stairwell as he walked to his bedroom late at night and there was some comfort in imagining it such before the truth of his life was torn apart again by gossip and conjecture.

He was alone and running from a past that kept reaching out, even here in a quiet, warm room and in the company of friends. Lifting the glass of brandy to his lips, he finished the lot.

'You look like a man who needs to unload his demons, Francis.' Gabriel said this, his voice close and worried. 'Adelaide thinks you have the same appearance as I did when I first met her, swathed in secrets and regrets.'

'How did she cure you, then?'

'Oh, a good wife has her ways, believe me, and mine was never a woman to give up.'

Lucien joined in the conversation now. 'It's

what you need, a woman with gumption, spirit and humour.'

'And where do you think I shall find this paragon that you describe?' The brandy was loosening his tongue and stilling the shakes and with the blanket about his shoulders he was finally feeling warmer and safe.

'Perhaps you have just done so, but do not know it yet.'

Francis frowned in sheer disbelief. 'Lady Sephora Connaught is engaged to be married to the only son of a duke. A slight impediment, would you not say, even given the fact I have not yet shared one word with her.'

'But you will. She will have to thank you for risking your life and I am certain jumping into a dangerous freezing river must have its compensations.'

'Is it the brandy that is making you both talk nonsense for I am damned sure that the so-called "angel of the *ton*" would have enough sense to keep well away from me?'

'You paint yourself too poorly, Francis. Seth Greenwood's cousin, Adam Stevenage, said that you had tried to save Seth. He said that you held him up out of the mud for all the hours of the day and it was the cold that killed him come the dusk.' Lucien said this softly, but with conviction.

'Stop.' The word came with an anger Francis could not hide and he turned away from the glances of both his friends. 'You know nothing of what happened at Hutton's Landing.'

'Then tell us. Let us help you understand it instead of beating yourself up with the consequences.'

Francis shook his head, but he could not halt the words that came. 'Stevenage is wrong. I killed Seth with my own stupidity.'

'How?'

'It was greed. He wanted to leave after the first lucky strike, but I persuaded him to stay.'

'For how long?'

'A month or more.'

'Thirty days?' Lucien stood now and walked to the window. 'Enough time for him to have changed his mind if he had wanted to. How long did you have to think about jumping into that river today?'

Francis frowned, not quite catching his drift, and Lucien went on.

'Two seconds, five seconds, ten?'

'Two, probably.' He gave the answer quietly.

'Did you think about changing your mind in those seconds?'

'No.'

'Well, Seth Greenwood had millions and millions of those same seconds, Francis, and neither did he. Would it have been our fault if you had jumped today and never resurfaced? Should we have languished in guilt forever because of your decision to try and rescue Lady Sephora Connaught? Are one man's actions another man's cross to bear for eternity if things don't quite turn out as they should?'

Gabriel began to laugh and brought the bottle of brandy over to refill their glasses.

'You should have taken to the law, Luce, and you to the ministry, Francis. Arguments and guilt have their own ways of tangling a man's mind and no doubt about it. But here's to friendship. And to all the life that's left,' he added as their glasses clicked together in the fading dimness of the library.

'Thank you.' Francis felt immeasurably better, lightened by a logic he had long since lost a hold of. He'd been mired in his guilt, it was true, stuck in the darkness like a man who had run out of hope and could not go on.

He had to move forward. He had to live again and believe that all he had lost could be found. Happiness. Joy. The energy to be true to himself.

He'd heard a voice, too, before he had jumped, from above or in his head he knew not which. A voice he knew and loved; a voice instructing him to save the girl in order to save himself and to be whole again.

God, was he going mad? Was this insanity the result of excessive introspection and guilt? Raising his glass, he drank of it deeply and thought that he had only told his friends the good half of a long and damn sordid story because the other part was too painful for anyone to ever have to listen to.

Chapter Three

Five days later his butler came into his library with a heavy frown upon his face.

'There is a gentleman to see you, Lord Douglas. From Hastings, my lord. He has given me this.'

Walsh passed over a card and Francis looked down. Mr Ignatius Wiggins, Lawyer. 'Show him in, Walsh.'

The man was small and dressed in unfashionable clothes of brown. He looked nervous as he fidgeted with a catch on the leather case that he held before him like a shield.

'I am the appointed counsel of Mr Clive Sherborne, my lord, and I have come to tell you that he has been murdered, sir, in Hastings a week ago. It was quick by all accounts, a severed throat and a knife to the kidney.

Good Lord, Francis thought. He stood to digest the brutality of such an ending and thought of the deceased. He had met him only once for he'd come to the Douglas town house with his wife, a garish but handsome-looking woman of low character and poor speech. They had come with the express purpose of informing his uncle about the birth of a baby whom they insisted was his by-blow. Wiggins had accompanied them.

Lynton St Cartmail had been furious and wanted nothing to do with such a hoax. Blackmail, he'd called it, Francis remembered, as he had ordered them summarily gone.

Clive Sherborne, however, had taken the child they had brought with them in his arms, a crying-reddened baby with dark lank hair and pale skin, even as he promised that he would instruct a lawyer to call on the fourth Earl of Douglas. His voice had been gentle and sad, a man who had not looked like the type to be murdered so heinously years later and Francis wondered what had happened in the interim to make it thus.

'Mr Sherborne had asked me to inform you of any significant events in his household, my lord, and so I am—informing you, I mean, about his death. A significant event by anyone's standards.'

'Indeed it is, Mr Wiggins.' Francis wondered briefly whether the mother, Sherborne's wife, was still alive and what had become of the girl child. He wondered why Wiggins had come back, too, given the amount of years that had passed since last being here.

'The deceased had given me a letter, sir, in better times, you understand, a missive that was to be delivered into your hands only in the circumstances of his death, for he wanted to make certain that Anna Sherborne was…catered for. He was most adamant that I should give you this last correspondence personally, my lord, and that I should allow no other to take my stead…'

Francis remembered Wiggins distinctly, for his physical countenance looked much the same as it had. Last time he had gesticulated wildly at the screaming bundle of the unwanted newly born baby, but this time his hands were clasped tightly together, dark eyes showing an ill-disguised puzzlement mixed with fear.

'I shall not be a party to the lies any longer, Lord Douglas. Your uncle, the fourth Earl of Douglas, Lynton St Cartmail, paid me well to keep my silence about his illegitimate daughter and I have regretted it ever since.'

'He paid you?'

'From his own private funds, my lord, and they were substantial. The receipts are all here.'

The horror of the lie congealed in Francis's throat. The thought of a child, who was in effect his cousin, lost under his uncle's profligate womanising, was so shocking he felt the hair rise along his arms. Lynton had laughed off the charade of her birth as an obscene pretension by a misguided harlot to gain money from the coffers of the Douglas estate and at twenty-two Francis had had no cause to think the old earl was being anything but truthful. He could barely believe the dreadful falsehood and struggled to listen as the lawyer went on.

'This is the end of it, you understand, and I won't be held responsible for the consequences. I am elderly, my lord, and trying to make my peace with the Almighty and this deception has played heavily upon my conscience for years.'

Opening his bag, he found a thick wad of documents, which he laid down on the desk. 'This is the missive Mr Sherborne left in my care. It outlines the Douglas monies accorded

to him for seeing to the child's upbringing and
also any extra amounts sent. I should like to
also say that although gold can buy certain
things, sir, happiness is not one of them. Unfortunately. Miss Anna Sherborne is now largely
at the mercy of the borough and one who has
no idea of the true circumstances of her family
connections and elevation.'

'Where is she now?'

'It is all there, my lord, all written down in
the letter, but…'

'But?'

'The child has been brought up without
proper rule of law and although Clive Sherborne was born a gentleman he most certainly
did not have the actions of one. His wife, God
rest her soul, was even less upstanding than her
husband. To put it succinctly, the young girl is a
hoyden, unbridled and angry, and she may well
need a lot more from you than the promise of
some sort of temporary and transitory home.'

Francis's head reeled, though he made an effort to think logically. 'Then I thank you for
your confidentiality and for your service, Mr
Wiggins, and sincerely hope you will bring the
girl here to London in the next few days for the

Douglas birthright should be her own.' He said the words quietly, the tremble of his hand the only thing belying complete and utter fury at his uncle as he paid the man off for his troubles and watched him depart.

Lynton St Cartmail's foolish and ongoing lack of responsibility had now landed firmly on his shoulders and the covering letter the lawyer had given him felt heavy as he ripped open the seal and looked down.

Anna Sherborne was almost twelve years old. He stopped, trying to remember himself at the same age. Arrogant. Cocksure. His parents had died together a few years prior in an accident so that could have been a factor in his belligerence, but Anna Sherborne's life had not been an easy one either and by the accounts of the lawyer she sounded…damaged.

The Damaged Douglas. That echo made him stand and walk to the window. What the hell was he to do with an almost-twelve-year-old girl? How did one handle a female of that particular age with any degree of success? God, no one had done so thus far in her life by all accounts and he did not wish to impair her further by his ignorance of the issues. His uncle must have known what would happen when he had turned his unsuitable lover and their offspring away with a good deal of financial support and an express intention never to see them again.

Well, she was his responsibility now. He'd need a governess, of course, some female relative with a firm and respectable hand to temper out all the knots and bumps expected in a wayward and abandoned child. He'd need patience, too, and honesty. And luck, he added, catching his reflection in the window.

Sephora Connaught's nail-marks had settled somewhat on his right cheek, though they were still easily seen in the glass, three reddened lashes running from the corner of his eye.

On the other side the scar from the Peninsular Campaign blazed. He saw others looking at it often, of course he did, this mark that cut his face in half, but he'd made the conscious decision years ago not to let it define him. Still there were times… His finger marched along the pathway of injury and he felt the loss of who he had been and what was left now.

He was supposed to be accompanying Gabriel and Adelaide Hughes to a ball tonight given in honour of a friend's father. Part of him wished he did not have to go out and be seen after the incident by the river the other day, but the more sensible part of him reasoned that if there was speculation directed at him then so be it.

A small bit of him also hoped that Lady Sephora Connaught might also be attending the ball. He wanted to take a look at her and see if what he remembered matched the truth of her countenance.

Perhaps it was Lucien's words alluding to her as the 'angel of the *ton*' that had coloured his reminiscences, but he had begun to imagine her in a way that could only be called saintly. She'd had light hair, of that he was sure, but her face in the water had been blurred and indistinct. He did know her lips were full and shapely because he had been focused upon them as he had allowed her his breath.

An intimate thing that, he supposed, and the reason for this ridiculous but abiding interest. He had kissed a hundred woman in his life and bedded a good number, but this was the first time he had felt…what? Connected? Haunted? Aroused with such a speed it felt improper?

All of those things and none of them. Walking to his room, he turned when his valet came in to lay out his clothes for the evening and cursed his mindless and maudlin sentimentality.

Sephora Connaught was to be married forthwith to the Marquis of Winslow and he was by all terms a great and worthy catch. Still, he looked forward to seeing the elusive daughter of Lord and Lady Aldford tonight at the ball even if it was just to understand that the power of reminiscence was never as strong as the reality of a cold hard truth.

Sephora did not wish to go to the Hadleighs' ball and she told her mother of it firmly.

'Well, my dear, it is all very well to be nervous and of course after the events of the past week it is only proper that you should be, but you cannot hide forever and five days of being at home is enough. Richard will be there right beside you as will Maria, your father and I and, if anyone has the temerity to comment in any way that is derogatory, I am certain we shall be able to deal with them effectively.'

Her mother's words made perfect sense, but for the first time in her life Sephora was not certain that anything would ever be all right again.

She was either constantly in tears or as tired as she ever had been and the doctor her mother had called had told her 'it was only by rejoining the heaving mass of humanity and partaking in social intercourse that she would ever get well'.

His words had left her sister in fits of laughter and even she for the first time in days had smiled properly, but when putting on her new lemon gown this evening with its ruched sleeves and silken bodice she felt dislocated and adrift.

Her leg had healed and she hardly noticed the pain of it any more, though the doctor had been adamant that she leave the bandage on for a good few more days yet. Richard had presented her with new earrings and a matching bracelet and she had worn these tonight to try and lift her spirits.

It was not working. She felt heavy and wooden and afraid and the diamonds were like a bribe for his lack of...what?

She could not bear to have him touch her, even gently or inadvertently. She had not caught his eyes properly either lest he see in the depths of them some glint of her own accusations. A coward. An impostor. A man who could not and would not protect her.

So unfair, she knew. He was unable to swim competently, as were a great many men of the *ton*, and he had done his utmost ever since to make certain that she was healing and happy. Large bunches of roses had arrived each day, and because of it all she would associate their smell with this dreadful time forever and hate the scent of them until her dying day.

Her dying day. That was the crux of it. She had escaped death by the margin of a whisper and could not quite come to terms with the fact. Oh, granted, she was here still, breathing, eating, sleeping, walking.

And yet…she wasn't.

She was still under that water, trapped in her heavy clothes and in the darkness waiting to die.

Her skin crept with the thought and she shivered. She felt as if she might never truly be warm again even as the maid placed the final touches to her curled hair with a hot iron.

She looked presentable and calm when she glanced at herself in the mirror a few moments later. She looked as she always had done before any ball or social event of note: mannerly, gracious and composed. She had never been criticised for anything at all until this week, until she had clung to Francis St Cartmail in her torn and sodden riding clothes as though her life had depended on it.

Well, indeed it had. She smiled and the flush in her cheeks interested her. She seldom had high colour and just for a moment Sephora thought such vividness actually suited her, made her eyes bluer and her hair more golden. Usually her skin held the sheen of a statue cut from alabaster, like the one of the *Three Graces* she had seen in an art book at Lackington's in Finsbury Square. Translucent and composed. Women untouched by high emotion or great duress.

Maria's noisy entrance into her chamber had her looking away from her reflection.

'The carriage is here, Mama. Papa and the marquis are waiting downstairs.'

'Then we shall come immediately. Have you a wrap, Maria? It is cold outside and we do not want a case of the chills. Sephora, make certain you bring your warmest cloak for there is quite a wind tonight and the spring this year has a decided nip to it. After the incident at the bridge we do not wish for you to sicken, for your body's defences will be lowered by the alarm of your accident.'

And with that they were off, bundled into the carriage full of Maria's happy chatter and her mother's answering interjections.

On her side of the conveyance Sephora simply held her breath, squashed as she was between her father and Richard, and wondered how long she could keep doing so before she might faint dead away. She had got to the slow count of fifty in her room before the black spots had begun to dance in front of her eyes. She did not dare to risk the same here. But still she liked the control of it, silent and hidden. A power no one could take away from her, an unbidden and unchallenged authority.

At least the ballroom was warm, she thought half an hour later, as their party made their way through the crowded rooms, this outing so far holding none of the fear she'd imagined it might.

'You look beautiful this evening, my dearest love,' Richard said as they took their places at the top of the room, the orchestra easily observed from where they stood. 'Lemon and silk suits you entirely.'

'Thank you.' There was a tone in her voice that was foreign and displaced.

'I hope we might have a dance together as soon as the music begins.'

Her heart began to beat a little faster, but she pushed the start of panic down. 'Of course.'

She was coping and for that she was glad. She was managing to be just the person everybody here thought she was. No one watched her too intently, no conversation had swirled to a stop as she passed a group, no whispered conjectures or raised fans behind which innuendo could be shared. No pity.

Her betrothed's first finger touched a drop of ornately fashioned white gold at her ear. 'I knew they would look well on you as soon as I saw them, my love. I was planning on keeping them as a surprise until your birthday, but you looked as if a present might be the very thing needed to cheer you up. I managed to get them at a good price from Rundell's as they have high hopes of my further ducal patronage in the future.'

'I imagine that they do.' She tried to keep sarcasm from the words, but wondered if she had been successful as he turned to look at her sharply. She had not used such a thing before, the poor man's version of humour, but tonight she could not help it. The chandelier above them gave the blurred appearance of light through water and it momentarily made her take in a deep breath.

All about her was a living, moving feast of life: five hundred people, myriad colours, the scent of fine food and the offer of expensive wine. Without thought her hand lifted to a long-stemmed crystal glass on the silver platter a footman had just presented to the party and if Richard frowned at her choice he had at least the sense not to say anything.

She seldom drank alcohol, but the orgeat lemonade tonight held no allure at all. It looked like the water of the Thames somehow, cloudy, cold and indistinct. She swallowed the wine like a person finding a waterhole in the middle of an endless desiccated African desert and reached out for another. Her mother shook her head even as Richard set his bottom teeth against his top ones and tried to smile. The glint of anger in his eyes was back.

But it was so good, this quiet escape that took the edge off a perpetual panic and made everything more bearable. Even the gaudy new bracelet twinkling in the light started to have more appeal.

The beginnings of the three-point tune of

a waltz filled the air around them and when her betrothed took her arm and led her into the dance she allowed him the privilege. His closeness was not the problem it would have been ten minutes earlier and she wondered if perhaps she had been too harsh on a man who after all had always loved her and had failed to learn to swim.

The feel of him was known, his short brown hair well cut and groomed, the smell of an aftershave that held notes of bergamot and musk.

'You look very pretty, Sephora, and more like yourself.' This time his smile was genuine and she saw in him for a moment the boy whom she had grown up with and played with, though his next words burst that nostalgic bubble completely. 'I do think, though, that you should refrain from imbibing any more wine.'

'Refrain when I have barely begun to feel its effect?'

'You have had two full glasses already, my dearest heart, and you are now in some danger of flippancy.'

'Flippancy?' She rolled the word on her tongue and liked it. She had never been flippant. She had always been serious and composed and polite until she had fallen headlong into that river and discovered things about herself that she could no longer hide.

For just a second she thought she loathed her intended groom with such ferocity she might well indeed have simply hit him. But the moment passed and she was herself again, chastised by the impulse and made impotent by fright.

Who was that inside of her? What crouched below the quiet and ladylike bearing that was her more usual demeanour and appearance, the lemon silk in her gown, the curls in her hair, the dainty bejewelled slippers upon her feet?

She had a headache, she did, a searing terrible headache that made her sick and dizzy. Richard in a rare moment of empathy recognised the fact and led her over to a chair near the wall apart from the others and made her sit down.

'Stay here whilst I find your mother, Sephora. You do not look well at all.'

She could only nod and watch him go, the slight form of him disappearing amongst the crowd to be replaced by a man she recognised instantly.

'You.' Hardly mannerly, desperately said. The

sound came from her in a whisper as Francis St Cartmail stood alone in front of her.

'I am glad to see you much recovered, Lady Sephora. I am sorry I did not stay to see to your welfare after…' The earl stopped.

'My drowning?' She supplied the ending for him and he smiled. It made his face softer somehow, the scar on his left cheek curled into a smaller shape and her three scratches on his right almost disappearing into a deep dimple.

'Hardly a drowning. More a case of getting wet, I think.'

Simple words that she needed. Words that took away the terror and the hugeness of all that had transpired. He was even looking at her with humour in his eyes. Sephora wanted him to keep on talking, but he didn't, though the stillness that fell between them was as distinct as any conversation.

'Thank you,' she finally managed.

'You are welcome,' he returned and then he was gone, Richard in his stead with her mother, her face creased in worry and remorse.

'I should never have let you come. I shall have a good word with the doctor after this and tell him that it was much too soon and that…'

The words rattled on, but Sephora had ceased to listen. She was safe again, she knew it.

Hardly a drowning. More a case of getting wet, I think.

She suddenly knew that Francis St Cartmail would never have let her drown, not in a million years. He would have jumped in and saved her had the depth of the water been ten feet or twenty. He would have dragged her across a current many times more dangerous or a river fifty times as wide if he had had to.

Because he could.

Because she believed that he could, this enigmatic and unusual earl with his wide shoulders and steel-strong arms.

The relief of it was so startling she could barely breathe. She smiled at the thought. Breath was the one thing she did have now here in the Hadleighs' ballroom under thirty or more elegant chandeliers and an orchestra of violinists beating out a waltz.

She was alive and well. The spark inside her had not been quenched entirely and was at this very moment bursting into a tiny flaring flame of revival.

She could not believe it.

Francis St Cartmail's smile was beautiful and the cabochon ring on his finger was exactly as she remembered it. His voice was deep and kind and his eyes were hazel, like the leaves fallen in a forest after a particularly cold autumn, all of the shades of ruin.

And people watched him, carefully, uncertainly, the wave of faces following him holding both fear and awe and another emotion, too. Wonderment, if she might name it as he stalked alone through a sea of colour and wearing only a deep swathe of unbroken black.

She hoped there was someone here he might find a shelter with, some friend who would throw off the *ton*'s interest with as much nonchalance as he did himself, but he was lost to sight and her mother and Richard observed her closely.

She did not want to go home now. She wished to stay here so that she might catch sight of the Earl of Douglas again and hope that another conversation might eventuate.

He'd smelt like soap and lemon and cleanness, the crisp odour of washed male having the effect of bringing Sephora quickly to her feet.

Her worried mother took her hand.

'Would you like some supper, my dear? Perhaps if you ate something you might feel better?'

Food was the last thing she truly wanted, but some sort of destination solved the problem of simply standing there dumbstruck, so she nodded.

After that most unusual exchange Francis went to join Gabriel Hughes leaning against a pillar on one side of the room. 'Was she what you expected?'

'You speak of Lady Sephora, I presume?'

'Cat and mouse does not suit you, Francis. I saw you talking to her. What did you think?'

'She is smaller than I remember her and paler. She is also frightened.'

'Of what?'

'I think she was sure she was going to drown and has suffered since for it. She thanked me for saving her.'

'And that's all that she said?'

'Well, there was some silence, too.'

'The stunned silence of Perseus falling in love with the drowning Andromeda?' Gabriel's tone held a good deal of humour in it that Francis ignored.

'She fell off a bridge, for God's sake. She was not chained to a rock waiting to be devoured by sea monsters.'

'Still, one must feel a certain connection when a soul is saved. I would imagine something along the lines of the life debt in honour-bound cultures, so to speak.'

'A heavy price, if that's the case? I did not see such in the eyes of Sephora Connaught, though they are surprisingly blue.'

Gabriel nodded. 'And young men have written sonnets about those orbs. The number of her suitors is legendary, though she has turned each and every one of them down.'

'For the marquis?' He didn't want to ask the question, but found himself doing so.

'Winslow fancies himself as something of an example others should be copying in both dress and manner, I think. He is said to be somewhat pompous and arrogant in his dealings with people.'

'Well, he looks fairly harmless.' Glancing across the room to where the young lord stood,

Francis saw that Sephora Connaught was tucked in beside him.

'Harmless but controlling. See how he positions himself at her elbow. Adelaide said that if I were to ever constantly hover like the Marquis of Winslow does, she would simply shove me in the ribs.'

'Perhaps Lady Sephora enjoys it?'

'I think she allows it because she has never known differently.'

Sephora Connaught's profile was caught against the light—a small turned-up nose, sculptured brow and cheekbones that were high. Her pallor was almost white.

'From all accounts Winslow congratulated himself quite heartily on his organisation at the riverside, but his bride-to-be does not look quite herself tonight. Perhaps she does not concur to the same opinion. Perhaps she wishes he had thrown caution to the wind and made the more solid gesture of self-sacrifice by jumping in after her.'

'Stop teasing, Gabe.' Adelaide swiped her husband's arm. 'It was a scary and dangerous situation and I am certain everyone tried to do their best. Even the marquis for all his pedantic and fussy ways.'

But Francis was not so sure. 'No, I think Gabe has the gist of him. Winslow sent me a card the next day. While he made an art form of thanking me for my help, he also implied that further correspondence with Lady Sephora would be most unwelcome. He did not want her bothered by any maudlin recount of the incident, he stated, and hoped I had put the whole nonsense behind me because he certainly had.'

'So you are now to be an inconsequential saviour? A man to be barely thanked?' Gabriel looked like he wanted to go over and knock Allerly's head off his shoulders.

'Winslow's father is ill so perhaps that is weighing heavily upon him.' Adelaide frowned as she added this to the conversation. 'It is, however, hard to imagine what a woman like Sephora Connaught might see in such a man.'

'She grew up with him,' Gabriel said. 'Both families are friends with strong ties and all adhere to the expectations of old tradition, so I am sure the parents are more than pleased with their daughter's choice of husband.'

As they watched, Sephora's well-endowed

mother, Lady Aldford, towed her away and he observed those around giving their greetings. What was it in the young woman that intrigued him? She was the *ton*'s favourite daughter, a woman who had managed to snag one of the loftiest catches of the Season without even a hint of criticism from anybody. People admired her. She was everything that was good and true and honest and she was beautiful along with it. Cursing, Francis turned away and was pleased when a passing footman offered around a new tray of drinks.

Chapter Four

An hour later Francis was standing by one of the tall and opened windows at the less crowded end of the room. He wished he could have gone outside to enjoy a cheroot, but oft-times at other balls he had been waylaid in the gardens by women wanting to share more than a word with him. Tonight he did not wish to chance it.

A hand on his arm had him turning and Sephora Connaught stood beside him, a look of pleading on her face and her voice low.

'I am glad to have this small fortune of finding you alone, Lord Douglas. I have written you a letter, you see, which I should have given you before when we spoke. The marquis let me know he had sent a card with our thanks, but I wanted the same chance myself.'

She bent to extract a paper from her reticule

and handed it over. 'Don't read it until you are home. Promise me.'

With that she was gone, tagging on the back of a group of giggling women walking past, her mother to the other side of the procession.

The older lady caught his glance at that moment and held it, steely anger overlying puzzlement. Tipping his head at her, Francis turned, the letter from her daughter held tightly in his hand.

Sephora hoped she had done the right thing by giving him her missive. Please God, do not let him show it to his friends so that they might all laugh at her, she prayed, as her mother's arm came through hers and Richard joined them.

She had not been able to leave Francis St Cartmail's bravery to the ministration of Richard's thanks. She owed him some sort of personal expression of her gratitude and her relief.

The fact that she hoped he might reply, however, made her squeeze her jaw together and grimace. It was the look in his eyes, she thought, that had convinced her to approach him, that and the blazing scar upon his cheek. He'd been hurt badly and she did not wish that for him. Even the scratches she had placed there herself were still visible.

Unfortunately she knew her mother had seen her speaking with the earl, but Elizabeth would say nothing of it within Richard's hearing distance. Maria was chattering away and laughing and Sephora was so very glad for her sister's joy in life. She wondered where her own joy had gone, but did not at that particular moment wish to dissect such a notion.

Over against the pillars on the other side of the room the number of beautiful women around Francis St Cartmail seemed to have multiplied. She recognised Alice Bailey and Cate Haysom-Browne, two of the most fêted debutantes of this Season, and both were using their fans with the practised coquetry of females who knew their worth.

'Have you enjoyed the night, Sephy?' Her father was beside them now and his pet name for her made her smile.

'I have, Papa.'

'Then it is good to see you happy after your awful fright.'

Just a fright now? She frowned at his terminology, thinking her parents had no idea of the true state of her mind.

'The marquis has decided to stay on for a while, but we thought to head for home. Richard has people to connect with, I suppose, now that his father is sick.'

'You saw the duke a few days ago. How does he fare?'

'Not so well, I am afraid. He and your Aunt Josephine are retiring to the country. I hope that he will at least get to experience the occasion of his only son's wedding in November before…'

He stopped at that and a constricting guilt of worry tightened about Sephora's throat. Uncle Jeffrey was a good man and he had only ever been kind to her, but she did not wish to shift her nuptials to Richard forward six months so that his father might live to see it. The very thought made her feel ill.

It was as if she stood on a threshold of change and to cross over it meant that she would never ever be able to come back. She was also unreasonably pleased that Richard would not be accompanying them homewards in the carriage this evening. Such a thought gave her cause to hesitate, but she could not explore the relief here in the glittering ballrooms of the *ton*.

Her mother was watching her closely and further afield she saw the wife of Lord Wesley, Adelaide Hughes, looking across at her with interest.

The cards of her life were changing, all stacked up in random piles, the joker here, the king of hearts there. A twist of fate and her hand might be completely different from the one that she had held on to so tightly and for so very many years.

The water beneath the Thames had set her free perhaps, with its sudden danger and its instant jeopardy. Always before this her life had flowed on a gentle certain course, barely a ripple, hardly a wave.

She was glad she had given Francis St Cartmail her letter, glad that she had mustered up the courage and seized the chance to do something so very out of character.

The Connaught wraps were found by the footman in the elegant entrance hall of the Hadleigh town house and moments later they were on their way home.

* * *

Francis poured himself a drink and opened the windows to one side of his library. Breathing in, he shut the door and reached for the pocket inside his jacket before sitting down behind his wide oaken desk.

The parchment was unmarked and sealed with a dab of red wax. There was no design embossed into it and no ribbons either. He brought the paper to his nose. The faint smell of some flower was there, but Sephora Connaught had not perfumed her letter in any way. It was as if the sheet of paper had simply caught the fragrance she wore and bore it to him.

He smiled at such fancy and at his deliberate slowness in opening it. Breaking the seal, he let the sheet of crisp paper unfold before him.

Francis St Cartmail...

Her written hand was small and neat, but she had made her 's' longer in the tail than was normal so that they sat in long curls of elegance upon the page.

His entire name, too, without any title. A choice between too formal and too informal, he imagined, and read on.

I should like to thank you most sincerely for rescuing me from the river water. It was deep and cold and my clothes were very heavy. I should have learned to swim, I think, and then I could have at least tried to rescue myself. As it was, I was trapped by fear and panic.

This is mostly why I have written. I scratched you badly, I was told, on your cheek. My sister, Maria, made a point of relating to me the damage I had inflicted upon your person and I am certain the Marquis of Winslow would not have made it his duty to apologise for such a harm.

It is my guilt.

I think that this rescue was not easy for you either, for Maria said you looked most ill on exiting the water. I hope you have recovered. I hope it was not because I took the very last of your breath.

I also hope I might meet you again to give you this letter and that you will see in every word my sincere and utter gratitude.
Yours very thankfully,
Sephora Frances Connaught

Francis smiled at the inclusion of their shared name in the signature as he laid his finger over the word. He could not remember ever receiving a thank-you letter from anyone before and he liked to imagine her penning this note, each letter carefully placed on the page. Precise and feminine.

Did she know anything at all about him? Did she understand what others said of him with the persistent rumours of a past he could not be proud of?

Leaning forward, he smoothed out the sheet and read it again before folding it up and putting it back in his pocket, careful to anchor it in with the flap of the fabric's opening. A commotion outside the room had him listening. It was late, past midnight and he could not understand who might arrive at his doorstep at this hour.

When the door flew open and a dishevelled and very angry young girl stood on the other side of it he knew exactly who she was.

'Let me go.' She pulled her arm away from the aged lawyer and stood there, breathing loudly.

'Miss Anna Sherborne, I presume.'

Eyes the exact colour of his own flashed angrily, reminding Francis so forcibly of the Douglas mannerisms and temper he was speechless. Ignatius Wiggins stepped out from behind her.

'I am sorry to be calling on you so late, my lord, but our carriage threw a wheel and it took an age to have it repaired. This is my final duty to Mr Clive Sherborne, Lord Douglas. On the morrow I leave for the north of England and my own kin in York and I will not be back to London. Miss Sherborne needs a home and a hearth. I hope you shall give her one as she has been summarily tossed out from her last abode with the parish minister.'

With that he left.

Francis gestured to the child to come further into the room and as she did so the light found her. She was small and very dark. He had not expected that, for both the mother and his uncle were fair.

She did not speak. She merely watched him, anger on her thin face and something else he could not quite determine. Shock, perhaps, at being so abandoned.

'I am the Earl of Douglas.'

'I know who you are. He told me, sir.' Her voice was strangely inflected, a lilt across the last word.

Removing the signet ring from his finger, he placed it on the table between them. 'Do you know this crest, Miss Sherborne?'

He saw her glance take in the bauble.

'It has come to my notice that you have a locket wrought in gold with the same design embellished upon it. It was sent to you after you left the house of your father as a baby according to the papers I have been given.'

Now all he saw was confusion and the want to run and with care he replaced the signet ring on his finger and took in a breath.

'You are the illegitimate daughter of the fourth Earl of Douglas, who was my uncle. Your mother was his…mistress for a brief time and you were the result.' Francis wondered if he should have been so explicit, but surely a girl brought up in the sort of household the lawyer had taken pains in describing would not be prudish. Besides, it had all been written in black and white.

'My mother did not stay around much. She had other friends and I was often just a nuisance. She never spoke of any earl.'

An arm came to rest upon a high-backed wing chair. Every nail was bitten and dirty and there was a healing injury on her middle finger.

'Well, I promise here you will be well cared

for. You have my word of honour as your cousin upon it. I will never ask you to leave.'

The shock that crossed her face told him she hadn't had many moments of such faith in her young life and she was reeling hard in panic.

'A word of honour don't mean much where I come from, sir. Anyone can say anything and they do.'

'Well, Anna, in this house one's word means something. Remember that.'

When Mrs Wilson bustled into the room on his instructions a few moments later he asked that the girl be fed, bathed and put to bed, for even as he spoke he saw that Anna Sherborne was about to fall over with tiredness. If his housekeeper looked surprised by the turn of events she did not show it, merely taking the unexpected and bedraggled guest by the arm and leading her off towards the kitchens.

'Come, dearie, we will find you something to eat for you have the look of the starved about you, mark my words, and in this house we cannot have that.'

When they were gone Francis's hands moved to the tightening stock about his throat as he walked to stand beside the windows. He needed air and open spaces for already his breath was shortening.

In the matter of a few days his whole life seemed to be changing and reforming into something barely recognisable.

First, he seemed to have won the eternal gratitude of the 'angel of the *ton*' and now he was guardian to a child who gave all the impression of being 'the spawn of the devil'.

Tomorrow he would need to find out more of Anna Sherborne's story and try to piece together the truth about Clive Sherborne's death.

But for now he finished his large glass of brandy and his fingers reached into the bottom pocket to feel for his letter. Pulling it out and straightening the paper, he began to read it yet again.

Sephora knew Francis St Cartmail would not write back. It had been days since the Hadleighs' ball and she understood the difficulties in receiving a letter as an unmarried woman. Still, part of her hoped the earl might have done so clandestinely via a maid. But nothing had come.

Maria had insisted that they walk after lunch

and although Sephora hadn't wanted to come this way she found herself on a path by the Thames, her sister's arm firmly entwined in her own.

'You look peaky, Sephora, and Mama is worried that you might never be right again. She has asked me to talk to you about the Earl of Douglas, for she thinks you might hold a penchant for him. She is certain that you gave him something the other night at the ball and I tried to tell her of course she is mistaken, but...'

'I did.'

Maria's words ground to a halt. 'Oh.'

'It was a letter. I wrote to him to say thank you...for saving me...for giving me breath... and to also say sorry for scratching his cheek so badly. The marks were inflamed and it was all my fault.' Stopping the babble, she simply took in a breath. 'I am glad I wrote.'

'And Douglas has replied?'

Sephora shook her head hard and hated the tears that pooled at the back of her eyes. 'No. I had been hoping he might, but, no.'

'Does Richard know about any of this?'

'That I sent a letter? Certainly not. He is...' She stopped.

'Possessive.'

'Yes.'

'How would Mama have known of it, then?'

'She saw me speaking with him at the ball.'

'You conversed with the Earl of Douglas? What did he say?'

'He implied that he would not have let me drown and that it was only a small accident. I believed him.'

'My God. He is…a hero. Like Orpheus trying to lead his beloved Eurydice back from death. The Underworld is exactly the same metaphor for the water and both rescues were completed with such risk…'

'Stop it, Maria, and anyway Orpheus failed in his quest.'

Her sister's laughter was worrying. 'When Richard holds your hand do you hear music, Sephora? Do you feel warmth or lust or desire?'

'To do what?'

'You don't?' Her whisper held a tone of sheer horror. 'And yet still you would consider marrying him? My God. You would throw your life away on nothing? Well, I shall not, Sephy. When I marry it shall be only for love. I swear it.'

Lust. Desire. Love. What pathway had Maria

taken that she herself had missed? Where had her younger sister found these ideas that were so very…evocative?

'I shall marry a man who would risk his life for me, a man who is brave and good and true. Money shall be nothing to me, or reputation. I shall make up my own mind without anybody telling me otherwise.'

'There are stories about St Cartmail that are hardly salubrious, Maria.' Sephora hated the censure she could hear in her words, but made herself carry on. 'A good marriage needs a solid basis of friendship and trust. Like Mama and Papa.'

'They barely talk to each other any more. Surely you have noticed that.'

'Well, perhaps not lately, but…' She made herself stop. Further along the river three men were walking towards them, three handsome men and one taller than the rest.

Lords Douglas, Montcliffe and Wesley, Francis St Cartmail's hair jet black against the light of day. He had not seen them yet standing against the sun and she debated whether to stay or to flee.

All Sephora felt was sick, caught here be-

tween truth and falsity, skewered in the teeth
of both hope and horror. She did not want this
suddenness. She liked things orderly and controlled. This was all so wildly unexpected and
so very worrying, but it was too late now to do
anything other than brave out the encounter.

He hadn't written back. Would she see the
distaste he felt for her upon his face?

'Smile, for God's sake.' Her sister's hard
whisper broke through fright and she did, pin-
ning a ludicrous grin across her grinding teeth
and beating heart.

'Ladies.' It was the Earl of Wesley who spoke
first, the urbane smoothness of his words prop-
ping up all the pieces that were scattering.
Sephora regathered her logic and straightened.

'Lord Wesley.' Her voice. Normal. She did
not look at the Earl of Douglas. Not even once,
but she felt him there, strong and solid.

'It is only by good chance that we wandered
this way.' Gabriel Hughes looked smug as he
said this. 'Montcliffe wished to have a view of
the river.'

Aunt Susan, her father's sister, had caught
them up by now, arriving from a good ten yards
back with her maid and a severe countenance.

She gave the impression of a mother goose about to do battle, but also sensing the high standing of its opponents.

Daniel Wylde, the Earl of Montcliffe, unexpectedly took her aunt's hand into his own and led her off to the side a little. Wesley seemed most intent on asking her sister questions about the weather of late, a topic she was certain he held no abiding interest in, which left her alone with Francis St Cartmail.

'I must compliment you on your letter, Lady Sephora. I have seldom been thanked with such profuse gratitude.'

His patronage made her prickly given he had not written back. 'Well, my lord, I have never been rescued with such valour and gallantry.'

'A stellar state of affairs then for us both, such a mutual admiration.' He smiled and the mirth touched the hazel in his eyes, lightening the darkness.

At his jesting, Sephora blushed a bright red, the colour sweeping into her cheeks and down onto her neck where no doubt it clashed violently with the pastel pink of her day dress.

She had always been so certain in every social situation, so very good at small talk and

mindless repartee. For the four years since her
arrival in society she had been measured and
polite and self-effacing. She had never uttered
a wrong word or a hurtful reply to anyone before. She had been careful and godly and good.
But not today. Today some other part of her long
hidden surfaced.

'Are you teasing me, my lord? Because if you
are I should like to say the incident for me was
beyond frightening. I thought I should not survive it, you see, and although I waited and hoped
for a reply you failed to send one.'

Oh, my goodness, why had she blurted that
out? She could even hear a note of pleading in
her tone.

'I am certain your mother would not approve
of any correspondence or indeed the—'

He stopped and she imagined it was Richard's name he was about to utter, but the conversation of the others came back to encroach
upon theirs. Aunt Susan was giving her good-
byes and, seeing such intent, St Cartmail did the
same, walking on amongst the greenery without looking back.

'Well, I have to say that was a lovely surprise,
would you not agree, girls. I knew Lord Mont-

cliffe as a young boy, you understand, as his mother and I were good friends, God bless her soul. I thought he may not have remembered me, but...well.' She smiled. 'He certainly seemed to.'

Maria squeezed Sephora's hand and they dropped back from the company of their aunt and her maid as soon as they were able.

'St Cartmail made you blush in a spectacular way...'

'Shh. Do not say a thing to Mama about this, Maria, or about my talking to the Earl of Douglas.'

'A bit late for that I think, sister dear. Aunt Susan will probably self-combust with the news the moment we reach home.'

'But if Mama asks you...'

'I will say we met their party purely by chance and enjoyed a quick and formal greeting.' Her eyes glanced down. 'Richard has not replaced your lost ring?'

Sephora shook her head and closed her hand across the lack of it, glad that her intended had not as yet noticed it missing. Something stopped her from simply marching into Rundell's and seeking a replacement herself for she had a good deal of personal money at her own disposal. But

she hadn't. She had not wanted to feel the ring
there with its physical promise of forever wind-
ing about her finger. The troth of being bound to
a man whose anger seemed to be rising monthly
and who seemed more and more demanding of
setting an earlier date for their wedding was also
disturbing. The only true emotions she felt now
for her big day were harried and scrambled. She
was glad it was still so far away.

Richard was waiting for her when they arrived home, his smile giving Sephora more than
a frisson of guilt. He looked tired today, heavy
shadows beneath both eyes and the lines on each
side of his mouth marked.

'I had hoped to walk with you, my angel,
but was held up.' The endearment she had once
liked now only sounded foolish and feeble and
she had to stop herself pulling away as he took
her hand in his and brought it to his lips. 'But
I must say the exercise seems to have brought
colour to your cheeks and you are looking even
more beautiful than you usually do. I hardly deserve such fairness.'

Maria's laugh was not kind and Sephora was

glad when her sister excused herself and disappeared upstairs.

Richard observed her departure. 'Maria is often morose, I fear, and I am glad you hold none of her countenance. I cannot even imagine how she will find a husband who could abide such dourness.'

The laughing, teasing truth of her sister came fully to mind as Sephora pulled away. Dour and morose were the very last words she would have used to describe Maria.

She was also aware of some dull and nagging pain that had settled in her chest, a heaviness that held her frozen. Even with a glance Francis St Cartmail could bring the blood to her skin, an energy bolt of feeling and frightening possibility that infused every piece of her body with a response. Richard had kissed her hand and all she had wished to do was to be free of him, to follow her sister upstairs and think about her meeting today with the Earl of Douglas in all its minute detail.

But the wedding preparations for their November celebration were going ahead. She even had the first fitting for her gown scheduled in at the end of the following month.

Trapped and breathless. The thought did come that she could simply run away and not have to face it. She was almost twenty-three, hardly a young girl, and wealthy in her own right, for her grandmother had bequeathed her a prosperous estate in the north as well as leaving her a generous cash settlement. The thought of just disappearing held a beguiling promise, but Richard was speaking again and she made herself listen.

'My father has asked that I bring you to visit him. He has stayed in town for a few days seeing a doctor. If it suited you, we could go now for I have a meeting in the mid-afternoon that I need to attend.'

She could hardly refuse to visit a man who had expressly asked for her company and so gesturing to her aunt that they would again be going out, she followed Richard to the waiting carriage, glad when Susan made no argument about accompanying them as chaperone.

Fifteen minutes later she sat with the Duke of Winbury in the sunny downstairs chamber of the ducal town house. He looked a little worse than last time she had seen him, more lethargic and less comfortable. There was a tinge to his skin, too, that worried Sephora and she was glad that her aunt and Richard had repaired to the other end of the sitting room, leaving them a little time alone. She had always liked Richard's father and perhaps in truth that was a small part of why she had agreed to marry his son in the first place.

He took her hand and his skin was cold.

'You look sad, my dear, and you have been so for a while now. Is everything all right in your world?'

'It is, Uncle Jeffrey.' She had called him such ever since she could remember, her parents and Richard's the very best of friends. 'I had a walk in the early afternoon with Maria and then arrived back home to find Richard at our doorstep delivering your message.'

'He is a busy man, is he not, with his politics and his desire to make a difference? Too busy to walk with you in the sunshine, perhaps? Too busy to smell the flowers and look up into the sky?' He smiled at her surprise. 'When illness strikes and you are suddenly confronted with the notion that the years you thought you had are no longer quite so lengthy, there is a propensity to look back and wonder.'

'Wonder?'

'Wonder if you should have lived more fully, made braver choices, taken risks.'

His voice was weakening with the effort of such dialogue and he stopped for a moment to simply breathe. 'Once I used to think the right path lay in work and social endeavour, too, just as Richard does. But now I wish I had seen the Americas and sailed the oceans. I would have liked to have stood on the bow of a sailing ship, the breeze of foreign lands blowing in my face, heard other languages, eaten different foods.'

Sephora's fingers tightened around Jeffrey's. It was as if this conversation lay on two levels, the spoken edge of truth hiding beneath each particular word. She did not want to be one day wishing her life had been other than what it was and yet here already she was considering other pathways, different turnings.

Could Richard's father feel this? Was he warning her? Uncle Jeffrey had asked for a moment alone and this was something he had not done before.

'You are a good girl, Sephora, a girl of honour, a girl any man would be proud to call his daughter. But...' At this he leaned forward and she did, too. 'Make certain you get what you need in life. Goodness should not mean missing out on the passion of it all.'

A coughing fit took him then and a servant on the far side of the room hurried forward to deal with his panic. Richard also came towards them, pulling back a little as if he did not wish for the reminder of sickness or for the messiness of it. He did not venture further forward, but waited for her to rise and come to him.

'I think we should go, Sephora.' He made a point of drawing his fob watch out and looking at the time. A busy man and important.

'Of course.'

Going back to Jeffrey, she explained their need to depart whilst Richard stayed at the doorway impatient to be gone. Her husband-to-be took her hand as she came up to him and placed her fingers firmly across his arm.

Mine.

The word came hollow and cold, an echo of uncertainty blooming even as she acquiesced and allowed him to lead her out.

* * *

Sephora dreamed that night of the water. She felt it around her face, the coldness and the dark, sinking and letting go.

In this dream, though, she did not panic. In this dream she could breathe in liquids like a fish and simply watch the beauty of the below, the colours, the shapes, the silence and the escape. Her hands did not close over her face and Francis St Cartmail did not dive in from above and give her the air of life, his tightly bound lips across her own.

No, in this dream she simply was. Dying, being, living, it was all the same. She felt the shift of caring like a scorching iron running across bare skin, changing all that was before to what it was now. And Uncle Jeffrey was there, too, beside her, sinking, smiling as he lifted his face to a breeze inside the water. Foreign lands and different shores.

Nothing made sense and yet all of it did. Permission to live did not only come from another saving your life, it also came from within, from a place that was hope and hers.

She woke with tears on her face and got out of bed to stand by the window and watch a waning moon. Once a long time ago she had often sat observing the stars and the heavens, but that was just another thing that had fallen by the wayside.

Once she had written a lot, too, poems, stories and plays, and it was only as she got older and Richard had laughed at her paltry attempts that she had stopped. She had not only stopped, but she had thrown them all away, those early heartfelt lines, and here at this moment she felt the loss keenly.

When had life begun to frighten her? When had she become the woman she was? The one who allowed Richard to make all the decisions and bided by all his wants and needs? He was a marquis now, but his father was ill. How much worse would it be when he became the Duke of Winbury?

She wiped away the tears that fell down across her cheeks because the thought of being his duchess made her only want to cry.

She felt vulnerable with such a loss of identity and at a quandary as to how to change it. If she talked to him of her feelings, what would she say? Even to get the words making sense would be difficult and he was so very good at laughing at the insecurities of others.

She was also more frightened of him than she had ever been, frightened of his overbearingness and his lack of compassion. Even with his father today he had been distracted, impatient even, and she had seen a look of complete indifference as Jeffrey had coughed and struggled for breath.

Her touchstones were moving, becoming fragmented. She no longer believed in herself or in Richard and the thought of marrying him no longer held the sense of wonder it once had. But still, was it her near-drowning that had brought things so dreadfully into focus, the want for a perfection that was as unreal as it was impossible?

She rubbed at the bare skin on the third finger of her left hand and prayed to God for an answer.

Francis spent the next few days going through every file his uncle had kept on the Sherborne family and there were many. He'd had them brought down from the attic, the dusty tomes holding much in the way of background on both Clive Sherborne and his unfaithful wife. There was little information on the child, however, a fact that Francis found surprising.

Anna Sherborne herself was languishing against the stairwell as he walked up to instruct his men which new boxes he wanted brought down. Her hair had been cut, he noticed, bluntly and with little expertise. It hung in ill-shorn lengths about her face.

'Did Mrs Wilson cut your hair?'

'No.' The word was almost spat out. 'Why would she?'

'You did it yourself, then?' His cousin sported tresses a good twelve inches shorter than she had done yesterday and her expression was guarded.

An unprepossessing child, angry and diffident. He sat himself down on the step at her level and looked at her directly, the thought suddenly occurring to him that he might find out a lot more of Clive Sherborne's life from questioning her than he ever could from the yellowing paper in boxes.

'Was Clive a good father to you, Anna?'

Uncertainly the girl nodded and without realising it Francis let out his breath.

'Better than my mother at least. He was there

often. At home, I mean, and he took me with him most places.'

'Did you have other brothers or sisters?'

'No.'

'Aunts. Uncles. Grandparents.'

'No.'

'Did Clive drink?'

She stiffened and stepped back. 'Why do you ask that?'

'Because he died in a warehouse full of brandy.'

One ripe expletive and she was gone, the thin nothingness of her disappearing around the corner of the dim corridor. But Francis had seen something of tragedy in her eyes before she could hide it, a memory he thought, a recollection so terrible it had lightened the already pale colour of her cheeks.

He took me with him most places. God, could the man have taken her there to the warehouse and to his appointment with death? Had she seen his killer? Had she seen the only man she knew as a father die? He shook his head and swore again roundly. At his uncle and at her mother. At the unfairness of the hovel Anna had been brought up in, at the loneliness and the squalor. She was angry, belligerent and difficult because in all her life it seemed no one except the hapless Clive Sherborne had taken the time to get to know her, to look after her. And now she was abandoned again into a place where she felt no belonging, no sense of safety, no security.

She'd cut her hair as a statement. *No one can love me. I am uncherished and unwanted.* His hands fisted in his lap as he swallowed away fury.

Well, he would see about that. Indeed, he would.

Chapter Five

This outing to Kew had been a mistake, Sephora thought a few days later as she walked with Richard, his second cousin Terence and his wife through the greened pathways of the gardens.

'Are you quite recovered from your dreadful accident? It was the very talk of the town.' Sally Cummings asked this in a quiet tone, her eyes full of curiosity.

'I am, thank you.' She didn't particularly want to discuss further what had happened to her at the river as she did not fully understand it yet herself and so was not at all pleased when Richard joined in the conversation.

'Sephora was left with only a small wound on her leg after all the fuss and that is quite cleared up now.' He tightened his grip on her arm. 'We were lucky it was not worse.'

She smiled tightly at this assessment of her health. Richard truly believed in the minimal effects the near drowning had left her with, but her hands still trembled when she held them unsupported and she had not slept properly for a full night since the fall.

Shaking away her irritation, she tried to look nonplussed. Richard had been most attentive on the drive here today, tucking a blanket around her legs and telling her how lovely she looked in her light blue gown. She knew this destination was not one he would have chosen on his own account and for that, too, she was grateful. It was Terence Cummings who had suggested the journey and she had assented readily because plants calmed her, the large expansive swathe of endless greens settling the air around her in a way the city never did.

Sally Cummings was usually quite a silent woman, but today she was chattier. 'You look happy here, Sephora. I heard Terence say the marquis was hoping that after your wedding in November you might venture to Scotland for a short while. The Highlands are renowned for their wonderful fauna and flora.'

'Scotland?' Sephora had not heard this mentioned before and turned to her husband-to-be. 'You thought to go there?'

Richard shrugged. 'Well, we cannot travel to Paris with all the problems in France at the moment and Italy is just too far away. I doubt I could spare so much time either, for there are things here I need to keep my fingers on, so to speak.'

'Of course.' The words were ripped from her disappointment. Just another plan that differed from what they had once discussed.

The older woman took her arm and tucked it into hers. 'Terence changes his mind all the time, yet if I do so even once he is most unhappy with me. It is the way of all men, I suppose, their need to be in charge of a relationship and the leader in the home. My father and uncle were both the same. At least you have known Winslow forever and that must be most comforting. A shared history, so to speak.'

Sephora was not sure comforting was the correct word to use at all as the number of years they had known each other wound around inside.

Richard was two years and three days older than she was. For much of that time they had celebrated their birthdays together, their parents making a point of adding two candles on the cake after she had blown hers out, so that he could have his own special occasion. A family joke with all the small traditions observed to consolidate a union and protect the considerable property of two important families whose land marched along shared borders.

She saw the tiny scar under Richard's chin where he had fallen from a tree when he was ten and the larger one on his small finger when glass had almost cut through the tendon at sixteen as he'd run from her in a game of hide-and-seek.

Memories. Once she had cherished them. How had that changed? Now when he was with her Richard often seemed like a man who had forgotten others had opinions that were also valuable and worthy. Sometimes, she thought, he barely even bothered any more with the pretence of listening to what she had to say.

Sally's voice came again through her musings. 'You are not wearing that beautiful ring Winslow gave you, I had noticed. Is it being cleaned?'

'She lost it in the river.' Richard answered, this time surprising Sephora, for she did not think he had noticed at all. 'That actually was the worst loss of the whole fiasco at the Thames. It was an expensive ring and now the fish are swimming with it.'

He laughed at his joke and so did the others, yet all Sephora could think of were his words.

'That actually was the worst loss of the whole fiasco...'

If they had been alone she might have said something, might have tried to make him understand how hurtful a comment like that was to her. But with Terence and Sally standing next to them there was no opportunity to question him and so she left it altogether, gathering her breath and looking around at the beauty of the trees in the gardens.

Shouting from behind had them all turning and a moment later a group of men came into view.

'Isn't that the Earl of Douglas?' Terence Cummings queried. 'What the hell is he up to?'

As he said this a punch was thrown. It was so far away Sephora could not see whether it was Francis St Cartmail who threw the first punch or one of the others, but then without warning the whole situation escalated into a full-blown fight, one man being laid into by the others.

'Should you help him, do you think?' Sally Cummings asked this of both men, but Richard shook his head.

'Douglas no doubt has had a lot of practice in such things. Let's see how he does.'

Terence Cummings nodded his agreement.

Sephora could now see Francis St Cartmail more plainly and although he was one against three it didn't take long for the others to begin to fall back.

Cummings was giving some sort of a running commentary, but she did not really listen. All she could comprehend was the hard knock of fists against faces, the sound of bone against bone and the shattering of flesh. It was not a fight as she had imagined them to be, not a boxing match or a ruled combat. No, this was more ferocious and untamed, the civilised world of the *ton* slipping back into a savagery of primitive masculinity. She could never in a million years have imagined Richard letting his emotions rule him in the way these men were.

Finally after a few moments those in the

larger group broke away and turned to disappear
into the trees from where they had come, leaving Francis St Cartmail alone to pick up his hat
and sling his jacket across his shoulders. When
he turned suddenly she saw the slick darkness of
blood around his lips. With his long hair loose
and the white linen of his shirt straining against
the sinew and muscle beneath he looked…un-
matched. His stance caught at her, his stillness
magnified by a gathering wind and the moving leaves behind him, a man caught in time
and danger, the white clouds scudding across
a cerulean sky.

And then he was gone.

'Just another one of Douglas's many fights
and disputes, I suppose,' Terence Cummings
drawled. 'The man is a complete and utter dis-
grace to his title and seems to enjoy flaunting
his skills in violence at every possible pass. He
needs to be taught a lesson.'

'Well, he did save Sephora the other day—'
Sally Cummings began, but Richard cut her off.

'He's a competent swimmer and it was not
far to the bank side. If one is proficient at something it does not make it such a risk.'

Terence's wife caught her glance at the retort

and then looked away, the undercurrent of poor sportsmanship on the Marquis Winslow's behalf evident in her frown.

But Richard had moved on now, in an opposite direction to the one St Cartmail had taken and all the talk was of the pagoda and the possibility of walking up its interesting and unusual oriental shape.

'You would not be able to manage it at all, Sally. You will need to stay at the bottom and wait for us.' Terence gave these words and his cousin nodded.

'Sephora can wait with you,' Richard said. 'She has never been one for heights.'

The anger that Sephora had felt just below the surface suddenly boiled. 'I think I could manage that.' She watched as a group of ladies and gentlemen came out of the entrance at the bottom of the structure. Many of them were years older than she.

'But Sally will have nobody to stay with her if you come.' Richard gave this in a tone of quiet reprimand, no thought or mention of Terence staying with his wife.

'Well, I do not wish to be a nuisance…' Sally's words were worried. 'It's just I have a prob-

lem with breathlessness and I shouldn't wish to
get only halfway up and not be able to manage
the rest of it.'

'Indeed you should not, my dear, for that
would be most disconcerting for all of us.' Terence patted her hand. 'Come, Richard, we shall
tackle the thing with as much speed as we can
muster and be back before you know it.'

And then they left, Sally Cummings's frown
the only remnant left of the altercation.

'Terence has his own worries at the moment
and so it will be most beneficial for him to take
this exercise. Winslow has his sadness, too, with
his father's ill health, I suppose.'

The day felt cooler as they walked around the
base of the pagoda and through the many scattered trees that had been planted to enhance the
vistas of the place. Sephora wondered whether
the Earl of Douglas had left the gardens already
and looked about to see if she could find any
sign of him still being there, but of course there
was none.

'I am sure Francis St Cartmail is long gone.'

Sephora had hoped that her interest was not
so easily read.

'You are not married just yet. Surely you are

able to still look at a man who is as unforgetta-
bly fine as Douglas most assuredly is.'

Without meaning to, Sephora laughed because Sally Cummings's statement was so unlike her more usual reticent uncertainty. As if
reading her mind the other woman began to
explain.

'I still have thoughts and a voice even though
Terence would prefer me not to have. I am sorry
to stop your ascent of the pagoda, but I needed
a moment to relax again. My husband is not
such comfortable company these days and I find
my nerves become most frayed. I am taking a
pill my doctor prescribed which should allow a
marked improvement to my disposition, but so
far I have just felt sadder.'

Like I do.

Sephora almost said this out loud, there in the
blue of the day and the green of the park, there
where Francis St Cartmail had fought with his
fists and with a passion largely missing now
from anything at all that she did.

Sally was six years older than she was and
looked twice that number. Would this be her
fate, too, in that many years again, walking here
in Kew and finding any excuse at all to avail

herself of half-an-hour's absence from a domineering spouse?

She was trapped somehow between expectation and her own inability to understand what it
was she wanted. Richard was safe and familiar
and if he was also dogmatic sometimes or overbearing, then were not all relationships based
on some sense of compromise? What married
couple had the perfect and flawless balance?

It could not be wise to throw away all that
was known and familiar for a shot at some
whimsical fantasy threaded with danger and
hope. Surely such was the way to ruin.

Smiling, she turned to Sally Cummings and
commented on the beauty of the gardens and
was glad when the other began to describe a
plant to one side of the small pathway upon
which they walked.

Chapter Six

Francis visited the Wesleys the next morning with the express purpose of procuring a salve from Adelaide Hughes for his split lip, so he was glad to find both husband and wife in the front room of their town house.

'We were just speaking of you, Francis.' Gabriel made that observation as he placed *The Times* on the table before him. 'It seems as if you were in a fracas at Kew Gardens yesterday and the doyens of the *ton* are not well pleased.'

'Winslow's gossip, no doubt. I saw him there.'

'Who the hell waylaid you and why?'

'Men who felt jeopardised because I was asking questions about the illicit supply of liquor.'

'Something to do with Clive Sherborne's murder then, I am guessing?'

He nodded. He'd told Gabriel the story of

Anna's guardianship and was glad that Gabriel had remembered, for it made things easier. 'His lawyer sent me a list of Clive Sherborne's enemies and it seems that they have taken up their old gripes against me. My ward is deathly frightened and I think she knows something of how Sherborne died, but is not saying.'

'My God. Are they likely to be back?'

Francis glanced across at Adelaide, who sat listening to this conversation with a heavy frown across her forehead. 'There is good money to be had in the handling of smuggled liquor. I thought I had been more than careful in my questioning, but...'

Gabriel shook his head. 'Lord, Francis, you are caught in the role of protector and getting crucified because of it and no way short of abandoning Anna to make it different. Your actions are the talk of the town and after the kerfuffle at Richmond you are becoming persona non grata to those mamas who may have thought you a good match for their daughters.'

'Thank goodness for that.' Francis took the tea that Adelaide had poured for him and smiled. He could not remember the last time he had drunk the stuff, though the taste was different from what he remembered it to be like as he took a sip.

'It's a new brew I have been experimenting with. The valerian root helps with anxiety and insomnia.'

'A medicine?'

'Tea began as that, Francis, but along the way it changed into what it is today. Anxiety comes from the absence of routine and peace in your life. You need a reason to settle down.'

He knew what they were going to say next and pushed the cup and saucer away from him as Gabriel spoke.

'We were saying that we ought to have an afternoon tea here. We thought perhaps Lady Sephora Connaught should be the first on that list.'

Francis felt the shock of her name, but stayed perfectly still. She'd been at Kew Gardens yesterday and he had seen the fright in every line of her body. He wished he had not. 'I think she is taken.'

'But not yet married.' Adelaide joined in the conversation now. 'Her lady's maid is my maid's sister and she is not at all certain the marquis is the one her mistress should be tying her hand to. She says that even before her near drowning

Lady Sephora had been restless and sad. There was talk, too, of a letter in her possession with your name upon it.'

'Lady Sephora wrote to thank me. There is hardly any scandal in that.'

'Perhaps she is a lot more than just grateful.'

'What are you saying, Adelaide?'

'All the things that you are not, Francis.'

He began to laugh. 'I have spoken to her for two minutes in total and have had a short correspondence from her once.'

'You have dragged her to the side of a swollen river, skin against skin, and from what Gabe has related to me given her the kiss of life whilst beneath the cold waters of the Thames. So I want to ask her to come to take tea with us this week. Would you like to join us, too? A small and select gathering.'

Adelaide watched him carefully as she asked this. 'I shall not be inviting the Marquis of Winslow, but I will invite Lady Sephora's sister. Lady Maria Connaught is an interesting young woman in her own right. Perhaps we might see if Mr Adam Stevenage could join our party as well for he is newly back from the Americas and I always found him intriguing.'

Gabriel brought his wife's fingers to his lips. 'I think you are in your element with match-making, Adelaide, though Francis here looks less than enamoured with the idea. Perhaps he should humour you, though, for it is my thought that such an endeavour lies akin to your medicine. Fix the body, fix the heart.' When they looked at each other and smiled, it seemed for a second that they'd forgotten they were in company. Francis envied them for that.

'It's my lip that I've ventured here to find some salve for, Gabe, not my heart.' The ensuing laughter wasn't comforting.

'Will you come, though, Francis? Please.' Gabriel's wife had a particular way of inveigling others to do her bidding and he was not immune to such persuasion.

'I'll be there.' His promise came quickly, but he wondered even as he said it if his choice was a wise one.

When he got home again he looked at the names he had listed that could have been implicated in Clive Sherborne's murder. He knew Anna was frightened of someone from her past and he needed to understand exactly who this enemy was so that he could protect her. Mr Wiggins's documents had made mention of a smuggling ring and that was where Francis had targeted his first questions, though it seemed every family in the village outside Hastings where the Sherbornes had lived were involved to some extent with the free-trade movement, and who could blame them.

The punitive taxes imposed by successive governments were becoming more and more onerous and the contraction of jobs on the Kentish weald had probably added its bit to the growing lack of legal employment in the area.

His finger wound its way down the surnames and occupations of those Wiggins had supplied him with. The parson, the quarryman, the local squire, the boatman, the butcher, the innkeeper. The list just kept on going.

In Kew Gardens his altercation had been with a father and his two sons who'd heard of his interest in identifying those involved at the London end of the supply chain. These three had purchased cut-price brandy and spirits on the side and were firmly of the opinion that anyone threatening their lucrative livelihood with exposure was to be scared away.

Well, at least they had the measure of him now and he knew that they had played no role in the death of Clive Sherborne for they hadn't recognised that name at all when he had asked them.

Still, it was a shame Lady Sephora Connaught had been there watching on, her pale blue dress stirring in the growing wind and a look on her face of pure and utter horror.

He smiled. Well, this was who he was, too, a man who would protect his own no matter what the consequences, an outsider, a lord who had never fitted in well to the narrow and confined world of the *ton*. It was best that she knew it.

Best that he did, too, with all these foolish notions of afternoon teas and refined polite conversation. He'd have to go to the occasion of Adelaide's because he had promised her he would, but after that...

He opened his drawer and pulled out the letter Sephora Connaught had written to him yet again. When he'd made certain that Anna was safe he would leave London and go north for his manufacturing businesses were calling out for more of his time and energy. Then he would repair to the Douglas family seat in Kent. He truly wondered if he would ever be back in town.

Sephora took an age to get ready for afternoon tea at the Wesleys, which was unlike her, changing this dress for that one and this hat for another. Her maid watched her with puzzlement as she finally stood in front of the full mirror in her room.

Usually she barely glanced at herself, but this morning she did, observing her shape and form with other eyes, hazel laughing ones, the gold in them pushed to the very edges of green and brown. The fight she had observed at Kew Gardens four days ago should have made her hesitant, should have underlined all the gossip that was whispered of the dangerous Earl of Douglas. But it had had the opposite effect entirely. It made her want to understand what drove him into such frenzy.

In the mirror the blue in her eyes caught the hue in her gown and her hair had been curled into a series of fair cascading ringlets. A hat sat atop that, a small jaunty shape that barely covered her crown. She had dabbed an attar of violets on her wrists and at her throat.

Please let the Earl of Douglas be there, a small voice entreated. She knew Lord and Lady Wesley and Francis St Cartmail were close friends and the hope of some sort of private meeting came to mind, a place where she might talk to the earl and understand what this obsession she was beginning to feel for him was about. It concerned her that she was thinking of him so much. She had never been compulsive about anything before and this new side of her personality was worrying, given her promised troth to Richard.

Maria was coming with her today, a fact that her sister was pleased about. 'I always wanted to see inside the Wesley town house, for they say it is one of the most beautiful in all of London. I hope that there are others attending who are not married, though.'

'Well, I am not married, Maria.'

'You nearly are. Unfortunately.'

Sephora had to laugh and it felt good to simply enjoy the sound. She also harboured a good deal of guilt given that her mirth was at Richard's expense, but she swallowed that thought down and vowed to enjoy the day. For once she was pleased to be free of constraint and righteousness.

She would tell him, of course, that she had been to the Wesley function without him, but if she did so after the occasion it would allow her the freedom to savour it first. Squeezing her fingers together, she was glad she did not wear Richard's ring and that it had been lost and never replaced.

Lost like a part of her had been. Her heart beat with a trip of apprehension as her sister accompanied her down the stairs and they walked outside to the waiting carriage.

The Wesley town house was as magnificent as Maria had heard it to be when they were shown in to a salon twenty minutes later.

The room was huge and decorated in a colour of yellow, which lightened it and gave it an airy otherworld feel, so unlike the darker and more sombre tones Sephora was used to. There were paintings on every wall and the furniture was of a French design, ornate and gilded, cushions of flowered tapestry sitting atop a row of chairs. The curtains were of thick gold velvet and tied back with colourful braided tassels. To one end stood a group of people chatting, though all noise stopped as soon as their names were announced.

Francis St Cartmail was standing by an opened French doorway talking with Lord Montcliffe and his wife. She caught his glance as soon as she entered, quick and covert, before it moved away. Almost angry.

Lady Wesley had taken her arm as she introduced them to everybody in the room. The only person she did not recognise was a young man with long brown hair who stood slightly apart. Mr Adam Stevenage. The name was somewhat familiar and Maria moved towards him like a magnet.

And then the Earl of Douglas was beside her, a good foot taller and much bigger in every way than Sephora remembered him to be.

'Lady Sephora.'

'Lord Douglas.'

Today his eyes in the light looked softer than they had ever before, though the brutal mark across his cheek did away with any prettiness at all and her scratches on the other side of his face were barely noticeable. She could glean no ill effects from the fight at Richmond save for puffiness on his lower lip.

'I had wondered if you would be here today.

I know you to be a friend of the Wesleys, of course, so I imagined perhaps I might see you and…"

She made herself stop. Why had she blabbered that out at him and with such a dull repetitiveness?

Taking two drinks from a tray that a footman offered, he gave her one. 'Gabriel's idea of the libation at an afternoon tea is very different from his wife's, thank goodness.'

The tipple was strong and Sephora coughed slightly, thinking of Richard, who only ever wished her to drink non-alcoholic punch or lemonade.

'Wesley buys his wine from the Cognac region in France and this particular drop rarely results in any sort of a hangover. I can vouch for that.'

She smiled, liking the way the wine was warming her resolve and making their meeting easier. She was glad, too, when he stepped further out into the gardened courtyard, giving her space and distance from the others present as she followed him.

He was just so very beautiful here in the sunshine, so beautiful she imagined she could simply watch him forever. With a sudden worry she pushed her fingers against her temple where the beat of her heart was thumping.

This is where it could begin, she thought, the scandal, the gossip, the stigma, here in this little moment in the afternoon sun because she wanted to throw herself into Francis St Cartmail's arms and never let go.

A length of darkness had escaped from the leather he tied his hair with and lay in a long curl across his forehead. She could very easily understand his attraction to all those women of the *ton* who spoke of him in hushed whispers inflected with an underlying blend of avarice and fancy despite his wildness and his danger.

When his eyes settled on her own there was something in his expression that made her speak.

'How did your cheek get scarred, my lord?'

The ice in hazel glittered. 'War is dangerous.'

'And no one fixed it for you?'

'I was lost in the Cantabrians. The army of Moore had rolled on towards Corunna so I had to make my own way to Vigo and by then...' He left the rest unsaid, but he did not turn his damaged face away from the sunlight and she liked him for that.

'Well, I think it suits you.'

'Pardon?'

'The scar. People will take notice of a man who has been through such pain and lived.'

For a second she thought he flushed at her words, but then the distance returned.

'England is a soft and gentle land, Lady Sephora. It is my experience that anything reminding its people of a consuming chaos in a faraway foreign skirmish is to be avoided altogether. You are the first person ever to ask me of it directly.'

'Everybody has their secrets, Lord Douglas, and if some are more hidden than others it makes them no less painful.'

He laughed, a throaty and hearty sound that held an edge of disbelief. 'They call you the "angel of the *ton*". Do you have any idea as to what they say of me?'

Frowning, she nodded. Indeed, she had heard of all the things that were told of him. Wild. Ill disciplined. Unlawful. Barbaric. Dangerous.

'I stood trial in America for the killing of a man.'

The shock of his words was great. 'Did you? Kill him, I mean?'

'No. Not that time.' All humour was gone now and in its place was bare fury.

'Then I am glad for it.'

'Why?'

'I should not wish to be indebted to a murderer for the saving of my life.'

'And are you…indebted?'

'I am, my lord. When you came to me beneath the waters through the cold and the dark I thought you were like a god.'

He shook his head, but she continued anyway, the need to tell him all of it and without anything held back so desperate.

'I'm to be married to a man who was also there on the bridge that day. The Marquis of Winslow. I am certain you know of him. He was the one on the riverbank who took me from you when you brought me to safety across the mud.' She waited till he nodded. 'But he did not jump in to save me. He did not risk his life for mine and I think…I think he was s-supposed to h-have.'

Horror marked her words, the truth of what she said to him out here in the blueness of the day so real and naked and terrible.

He touched her then, his hand gentle across her own, as though reassuring her. But it did none of those things because in the shock of his touch other truths surfaced, big important truths that Sephora could no longer deny.

She felt changed and heightened and alive. She felt unconstrained and sensual and womanly. It was as if in the company of the disreputable Francis St Cartmail she was someone else entirely, the person she might have been had she not let fear and propriety rule her.

I think I could fall in love with you.

My God, had she just said that out aloud? The horror of such a possibility kept her rooted to the spot waiting for his mirth. When his expression did not change she felt a relief so great she imagined she might fall down, down into a crumpled heap at his feet, clinging to his fine and well-polished boots.

The arrival of her sister, though, took the attention from such a dreadful possibility, Maria's smiling and cheerful face so opposed to all that was transpiring here. Sephora was very glad when a warm arm threaded through her own.

He was making such a hash of this, but with Sephora Connaught half a foot away from him and her blue eyes pale and kind, all the things he had thought to say to her were gone from his head and he was left…reeling. She had not mentioned seeing him at the gardens and for that he was grateful, but his time alone with her was running out like sand through a glass, each grain precious and draining away.

Mr Adam Stevenage was drinking hard and Francis watched as the young man finished his next glass and came over towards him. The sister, Maria, looked stretched and tense as she gave Sephora her greeting.

He could usually read people easily, but Sephora Connaught held so many conflicting emotions upon her face and in her eyes, that in the end he could discern only a cloudy wariness.

When he had touched her a moment ago it was as if an electrical energy had been transferred between them, a jolt of such proportion he had seen her pupils dilate. He wondered if his had done the same.

He wanted to try it again. He wanted to take her in his arms and feel the warmth of her lips again under his…

'Pardon?' Stevenage had asked a question directly of him and he had no idea as to what had been said.

'I just enquired, Lord Douglas, what you

thought of the town in Georgia called Hutton's Landing?'

'Why would you wish to know this?' Francis answered quietly, a sense of alarm growing.

'My cousin was there, you see, last year. I hoped you might give me your account of the place.'

Could Adam Stevenage's question really be this naive? Could a man with his own clear demons of drink not have heard the slander that circulated still about his time at Hutton's Landing?

'I think, sir, it is a town to be avoided altogether.' Francis hated the anger in his voice and the flat tone of memory that slithered beneath. He hated, too, that Sephora Connaught had turned to observe him and was able to see exactly what it was that he had always hidden from others.

There was tightness at his throat and the need to gulp in large breaths full of air. His hands fisted at his sides and he couldn't stop the shaking that emanated from them.

'You asked me to tell you of the flowers here in the garden, my lord.' Sephora's voice came through the growing haze and when she shepherded him across the lawn to a small grove of shrubs and perennials he followed. Away from the others she spoke quietly.

'Can I find you help? Your friends perhaps…?'

'No.'

'Then humour me whilst I try to discern the names of these plants, my lord, for whilst I am no true gardener it might at least give you a moment or two to recover your wits.'

'Thank…you.'

He listened to her voice, soft and musical, describing the scientific classifications of the shrubs. Even he knew that a lavender bush did not quite look the same as the one she insisted it was, but she was most convincing in her feigned interest and teachings. Certainly Stevenage had given up on further conversation and gone inside as had the younger Connaught sister, leaving them alone again out at the far end of the lawn.

He felt better now, more in control. He could not believe that the panic had come on so quickly for it never had done that before.

God. She would think him teetering on the edge of madness and mental incapacity for he had also been like this on the bank of the river Thames.

He wanted to be sick.

'I was buried…in mud on the side of the Flint River in Hutton's Landing. Sometimes the memory of it comes back.'

He had barely told anyone of the experience and couldn't believe he was now telling her. Still he could not seem to stop. 'I got out, but my friend didn't survive it.'

And he'd been hauled up for his murder, the rope around his throat and mud caked in his mouth, the hatred of the crowd of people who had gathered easily discerned. 'Hang him. Hang him. Hang him.'

'Do you think Adam Stevenage knows?'

This time his smile was more real. 'Yes.'

'Could he be dangerous…to you?'

Reason flooded back and he shook his head. He did not want Sephora Connaught pulled into his shadows. Out here with the light in her golden hair she did indeed give the impression of goodness and purity. The 'angel of the *ton*'. He was beginning to realise just how aptly she was named.

'Come, let us go inside.'

He was glad when she followed him in and even more glad when her sister crossed the room to stand beside her and garner her attention.

When Gabriel offered him a drink Francis took it.

'She is very beautiful, this small and pale Lady Connaught.'

'Yes.'

'And sensible, too. Are you feeling better?'

Looking up, he caught the concern in Gabriel's eyes. Gabriel had been a spy once and managed to see all that others thought hidden. 'She was trying to protect you out in the garden and in her fragility there is also strength. She does not wear Winslow's ring. I wonder why?'

'Stop.' The word came without hope for Francis knew exactly what it was Gabriel was doing and what he himself had thought to do. But it was all too dangerous and Sephora needed to be protected. He could not stay here. It was wrong and he did not wish to hurt her.

'Will you give Sephora Connaught my goodbye? And also my thanks to your wife?'

'Of course.'

'And inform Stevenage I will see him tomorrow at my town house. At one. Tell him to make certain he is not late.'

* * *

When Sephora turned around again the Earl of Douglas was gone. Part of her wanted to simply walk out of the house and follow him, but she shook that thought away and concentrated instead on what Adelaide Hughes was saying.

'When is your wedding to be held?'

'In November, Lady Wesley. In London,' she added and hoped no more on the subject would be said. But she was to be disappointed.

'It must be hard on you, waiting so patiently for a man you love with all your heart and soul.'

Sephora could not get the next words out no matter how hard she tried to. Marriage to Richard would not be the 'all heart and soul' sort, she thought to herself. It would be far more ordinary than that. She would not see oceans or walk on different lands. She would have babies and get old beside the first man who had ever kissed her and that had been done without the passion she had imagined should have been present. It was as much as she could in all honesty hope for. The thoughts she had had of Francis St Cartmail earlier burned underneath her conscience and she shook them away with fervour.

* * *

Francis spent the afternoon in the alehouses along the banks of the Thames, drinking and listening and asking questions.

One man had heard the name of Clive Sherborne and he dredged up more as Francis offered him a few coins to jog his memory.

'He always had a young girl with him, his daughter, I think, but he used to administer a sharp slap on her cheek every time she annoyed him and in the end she rarely spoke. He was selling cheap brandy, if I recall rightly, but I was not in the market for any of it as my wife's the one who does the books and she's a devout churchgoer. Nothing below the board, you understand, nothing that can lead to any trouble.

'I do remember, though, Sherborne held two prices for his contraband and I wondered when I heard he'd been killed if it was that which had seen him off. When I did buy on the occasion, for myself so to speak and private like, I remember it was the girl who put the coin in her pouch after counting it out.'

A picture of his cousin was beginning to form. A child dragged into the seedy underworld of contraband and men who would have no qualms in killing her for the gold that she carried. And Sherborne had struck her time and time again when she'd irritated him. No wonder she stood back and away from others. No wonder she peered out at the world with eyes that had seen too much hatred and known too little love.

If she had seen the final hours of Clive Sherborne's life, had the one who had done away with him known that she would be there, too, her father's follower, the helper who dealt with the money and counted it out? Would he be wondering right now where she was and if the girl had seen him? Could she be in as much danger as Clive had been, the next mark to ensure eternal silence?

Cold wrath began to settle inside his chest. Anna was his family, his responsibility, and as her guardian he would never let her be hurt. He was crossing off names on lawyer Wiggins's list, but he was nowhere yet near the name of the one who had killed Clive Sherborne.

'Not for long,' he whispered into the semi-darkness as he walked along the cobbled street. 'One mistake and I will have you, you bastard, and you won't even know what hit you.'

Chapter Seven

'**W**as that not just the *most* wonderful afternoon Sephora?' Maria laid her head back against the seat of their carriage and sighed. 'Mr Adam Stevenage is the *most* interesting man I have ever met, though perhaps in truth your Lord Douglas is the *most* beautiful.'

'Hardly mine.' Sephora ground the words out and her sister laughed.

'Every man you have ever met has fallen completely in love with you. Why should he be any different? You only have to forget the boring Marquis of Winslow and want him instead. You used to be braver once. You used to take risks.'

It was true, all that Maria said, but she had become more and more isolated as the years had fled by, careful of this, worried by that, cautious of a temper that Richard was having more and more trouble hiding from her.

But to just let go of everything on a whim and for a man who had not said a word that was even vaguely intimate? Oh, granted, Douglas had smiled at her and taken her hand, but he had almost certainly taken the hands of many other women in his time and more. She remembered the kiss she had observed in the garden at a long-ago ball, Francis St Cartmail's fingers wound into the hair of the well-endowed woman who had pressed herself to him.

Other worries also surfaced. What was it he had replied when she had asked if he had killed a man? *'No, not that one.'* The connotation that there had been others he had done away with hung heavily on her thoughts.

Yet Richard no longer represented safety or protection and the sum of all the other parts of him did not amount any more to enough.

Enough?

Everything had changed. Her perception of him, her trust in him, her conviction and faith in the future with a husband who would have simply let her drown.

'You think too much, Sephora.' Maria was

looking at her when she turned. 'You overimagine things. I can hear your brain going around and around from here. Why don't you just…feel and follow your heart?'

'Because people depend on me. Because Richard has been a friend since as long as I can remember and he would be hurt if…' She stopped, horrified by the confession she had very nearly given.

'If you broke off the engagement and told him the truth?'

'The truth?'

'That you fell out of love with him a long time ago, but are too kind to say so.'

'His father is dying…'

'And you are, too. Inside. Mama and Papa are just so pleased that you are marrying a man who may soon be a duke they fail to see your sadness. Today at the Wesleys you looked different. Francis St Cartmail makes you look happy again and if you cannot see the honesty in that, then…'

Her voice tailed off as she leaned forward, looking out of the window. 'The Winbury carriage is outside our place. Were you expecting Richard this afternoon?'

Sephora shook her head. Five thirty. Too early for him to be calling for the evening and she had supposed him to be busy in a meeting all day with his father's lawyer.

'But what is even more odd, Sephora, is that Mama is by the window watching out for us and she looks most upset.'

Through the glass Elizabeth Connaught was using a large kerchief to dab at her face and there were other shapes behind her. A quick burst of fear tore through worry. Was her father ill? Was Uncle Jeffrey worse?

A long time later Sephora would look back on this moment and realise that none of her concern had been for Richard himself; a telling omission, that, holding the portent of all that would come next.

But for now the footman opened the door of the carriage and they walked up the steps and into a house filled with the agony of grief.

Richard came towards her in the blue salon, his brown eyes reddened. 'Papa died an hour ago, my dearest.' His hand took hers as he said this and he squeezed it. 'All I can think of, Sephora, is that I am so glad you are here with me. Together we can overcome such sadness whereas alone it is something that I might not weather.' He almost sobbed out the final words.

He had loved his father and she had, too. The duke was a good man, a true man, a man who had been kind and honest and honourable. Tears of grief formed in her own eyes and fell unstopped and Richard simply placed his arms about her and brought her into his chest while pledging his love.

'We have each other, my love. We can survive this. I promise. Papa would have wanted that.'

Her parents, usually stalwarts for propriety, had both looked away, lost in their own sorrow, whilst Maria stood there wringing her hands.

'I am sure we can, Richard.' Sephora thought her words did not contain quite the emotion her groom-to-be wanted and needed to hear, but she simply could not dredge up more.

It was all so confusing. Here, in the heart of a great emotion that should have brought them closer, she could instead feel herself spinning away, like a top on the street, the string broken and all connection lost.

She also knew she could tell them none of it, Richard, her parents, Maria, not now with the dreadful news of Uncle Jeffrey's passing and all the associated protocols that would roll out over the next few days and weeks.

A ducal funeral.

She would have to be there for Richard. They would return to the Winbury country seat, no doubt, and she would have to stand beside him and act as a suitably loving and solicitous companion.

There was no other choice.

Richard's strong musky perfume only made her head ache.

'I shall not listen to what you say. I do not have to walk like this or talk like this if I do not want to and I shall most certainly not be wearing that.'

Francis listened to the shouts in the hallway from the safety of his library an hour later. His cousin's increasingly frequent temper and tantrums sat over his house like a great dark cloud, leaving him with no true idea as to how to deal with a moody, unhappy girl. As little, anyway, as the governess he had employed, he ruminated, thinking that something would have to change and quickly.

Mrs Celia Billinghurst had come highly recommended and she had the added advantage of being his late aunt's cousin. A distant relative admittedly, but still... She had all the credentials for a credible and skilled governess and yet her small charge was simply running rings about her. He should interfere and discipline Anna, but he found himself standing still until the argument dissipated.

The day had started badly and was ending worse and all he wanted to think about was the kindness of Sephora Connaught in the garden. He shook his head and stood, remembering the touch of her hand and the shape of her lips and the pale blue eyes watching him with the same shock of connection that he himself had felt.

She was to be married. She was the product of an upbringing in the *ton*. She was far too good for him, with her honour and honesty and kindness. It was this reasoning that had made him walk away from the Wesleys' town house today.

Tonight, though, there were other arguments that were more compelling. Never once had he felt so attracted to anyone—until now with the good and pale Lady Sephora Frances Connaught.

Why had he not met her before? She wasn't newly come to the *ton* and he had been back from the Americas for a good seven months already. Granted, society had held less and less appeal to him, but he had not caught sight of her at any of the balls he'd attended, he was certain of it. Their paths had just never crossed.

When he'd thrown himself off the bridge he'd not truly seen her either, just a flash of blue and a startled scream of shock. Her hat had flown from her head and rolled in the wind, a small and pale piece of wispy felt and netting that held her stamp upon it.

But now, he could not get her visage out of his mind or the feeling of her against his skin. Hell. He opened the window above him wider. Deciding even that wasn't enough, he grabbed his jacket and hat and strode off into the evening.

Outside and walking the edginess lessened. It was getting late, he knew that, but still he did not turn for home.

White's was busy when he reached it and a stiff brandy beckoned. Inside he found Adam Stevenage drinking. Without thought he slipped into the seat opposite the lone young man and simply sat there.

'You want to know why I asked about Hutton's Landing?' Despite the liquor Stevenage had consumed, he still seemed in reasonably good shape.

'The thought did cross my mind.'

'The man who died with you, Seth Greenwood, was my cousin.'

'I see.'

'And I wanted to know exactly what happened, to be able to lay him to rest, so to speak.'

'Surely you have heard the rumours?'

'I have, but I also think there are some things left out, my lord. I knew him well, you see, and one thing I could have said of Seth was that he was not careless. I also knew Ralph Kennings.'

That name ripped across Francis's composure, but he sat still and listened.

'I went to Hutton's Landing to visit my cousin's grave. I tried to find you there, but you had left the town. Into the bush, they said, with your gun. Ralph Kennings's body was found a few weeks later thrown into one of the many canyons and he'd been shot three times, twice in each kneecap and once in the head by a marksman. Had you not served in the British army in such a capacity, my lord?'

'It's a long way to Hutton's Landing, Mr Stevenage, and a long time ago.'

'Let me understand it, then. For Seth's sake.'

Francis was amazed that this talk had not made him breathless as any mention of Hutton's Landing usually did. Perhaps it was just the sheer overtness of Stevenage's questions, his quest for the truth overcoming everything else. Or perhaps it was just that Francis's body had already been once through the rigours of memory today and did not have the reserves to do so again. Whatever it was, he sat back and was once again on the banks of the Flint River in Georgia, the cooling of winter in the air and the southern edge of the Appalachians blue in the distance.

'We'd made a claim for gold and found a rich seam, Seth and I, and then found another that needed looking into. We'd fashioned a belt to put the scrapings on, one that ran up onto the river bank and saved us a lot of back-breaking work. It was going well until Kennings turned up and wanted a piece of it.'

He could see the structure in his mind, the

wood and the planks, the tailings of rocks and the glinting show of gold in the sieves after the water had sluiced the mud away. 'He knew that the venture was beginning to be lucrative and Seth was not one to stay silent about any new find.'

Stevenage shook his head. 'That sounds like my cousin. He was always an adventurer, seeking a life far from the ease of all that he had in England.'

Francis nodded. 'We were on the dredge when the whole structure collapsed and the next moment there were gunshots across the water. One of the bullets hit Seth in the shoulder and as it had rained the tide was rising. I held him up against me until he stopped breathing.'

'For most of the hours of the day, I heard.'

Francis didn't answer him.

'They told me you had paid for his gravestone, too. My family should be thanking you.'

Adam Stevenage had more than a small resemblance to Seth and Francis relaxed back into the seat as the other continued talking.

'I was glad to see you today, Douglas, at the Wesley luncheon, for I had been wanting to talk

to you and you're damn hard to pin down. Lady
Maria told me that her sister is to be married.'

'Indeed, she is. To the next Duke of Winbury.'

'I know that now. She just didn't have the
look of a woman in love. At least not in love
with Allerly.'

'I think you have probably said enough, Stevenage.'

The other lifted what was left in his glass and
made a toast. 'To gold then and to the truth.'

'Gold and truth,' Francis gave back and
drank. They could both of them break you into
tiny shattered pieces because the shades inside
each held so many different meanings. Seth's
boasting. Kennings's greed. His own retribution. There was a trick to getting away from the
fever before it took your soul and none of them
had mastered it. But Stevenage was not finished
in his confidences.

'Winslow's father died earlier this afternoon,
Douglas. Had you heard? He's now the new
Duke of Winbury. The *ton* has rules for it, you
see, for loving and living and dying and Lady
Sephora Connaught will be caught up in it like

a small leaf in a strong breeze. Hard to get away and impossible to break free.'

'You are drunk, Stevenage. Let me take you home.'

'You'd do that for me?' The younger man's dark eyes were pained, his own undisguised ghosts dancing within them.

'I would. Come on.'

'I am supposing that meeting you tonight nullifies the appointment Wesley instructed me to keep tomorrow at your town house?'

'It does.'

An hour later Francis arrived home to find a small pile of stones sitting in a careful order on the sideboard. Ordinary stones found in a garden or on any city street, each polished and arranged in size and colour. Had Anna placed them thus? He picked up the biggest one and rubbed the smoothness in his palm. He'd collected rocks, too, as a child and he wondered if he might be able to find the bags of his collections somewhere in the attics here. His cousin might enjoy them or she might well toss them back in his face.

He smiled at the thought and felt for the letter Sephora had sent him, liking it there in the warmth of his deep jacket pocket.

A surprising day of contrasts and truths. For the first time in a long while he looked forward to tomorrow, though the death of the Marquis of Winslow's father worried him more than it ought to have given Stevenage's prophecies. Would Sephora Connaught marry him out of pity? Or even duty? Outside the wind was strengthening.

A movement at the doorway had him looking up and there was Anna Sherborne, her hair tonight trimmed even shorter than he had seen it last week. She had been bathed, too, and dressed in her night attire she looked a lot younger than she usually did, although the scowl was ever present.

'I liked your stones on the hall cabinet. Did you polish them yourself?'

The girl did not come further into the room, but stood there straddling the doorway, one foot in and one foot out ready to run, he thought, ready to flee.

His eyes glanced at the clock to one side of the room. 'You are up very late?'

'I never sleep very well.' She offered this, tentatively.

'Neither do I,' he gave her back. 'Sometimes I sit and just watch the moon and I find that helps.'

He leaned forward and found a jar of toffees he kept in his drawer, taking one for himself and opening the wrapper before putting it in his mouth. 'Would you like one, too?'

He was careful in his offering, no importance at all attached to her acceptance or to her refusal. But she came forward and took a sweet, unwrapping it in exactly the same way that he had done and laying her paper down on the desk next to his.

'There is a lot more food in this house than there ever was at my old one.'

He stayed silent.

'Clive used to say that I was too expensive to keep and that if I had not been able to count well he would have put me out a long time ago.'

Francis stilled. 'What did you count for him, Anna?'

'His money. There was either a lot of it or none.'

'And he couldn't count it himself?'

'Some people can't. It doesn't mean they are dumb, it just means their brains are better at other things.'

'What was Clive better at?'

She didn't answer for a long time and then changed the topic completely.

'Clive said if you dug hard enough anyone could be buried. He said the old earl dug shallow holes.'

Blackmail, Francis thought. It came in the most unexpected ways and explained a lot about the many boxes the old earl had kept. His cousin had been the pawn in it, her whole life an extension of other people's greed and shame. But not his.

'I have my own collection of rocks, Anna.'

She looked up at his use of her Christian name and he saw a look he had not seen in her dark eyes before. Hope.

'I shall find them tomorrow and you would be most welcome to have them. Some are valuable, but most are there because I like them.'

'I do that. I collect what I like, too.'

A shout from further afield had her turning and his young cousin's maid, looking less than happy, came into view.

'I am sorry, my lord. I just saw her bed was empty and I have been looking everywhere…'

The servant looked as though she would burst into tears at any moment and his own expression was probably not helping either.

He wished he had had more moments of uninterrupted conversation with Anna. He wished she might have said more so that he could place the pieces of her life thus far with an added certainty into a pattern.

She liked counting. She enjoyed collecting rocks and he would bet his bottom dollar on the fact that she knew Clive Sherborne was being paid well to keep her. She had never once spoken of her mother and that omission in its own right was telling, too.

As the maid hurried her off Anna tipped her head at him before she turned and his heart warmed at the faint expression of acknowledgement and communication.

Francis saw Lady Sephora Connaught by chance seven days later dressed in the deepest of blacks and standing with the new Duke of Winbury and his mother next to a carriage pulled up in front of the St Pancras Parish

Church in Euston Road. Perhaps it was some sort of remembrance service, he thought, for he had heard the old duke's body had been taken back to the family estate for burial, the night funerals of London deemed too dangerous.

Sephora's hand was upon Winbury's sleeve, close and intimate, and he was leaning down slightly to speak with her, the sun in her golden hair contrasting against the hue of their clothing as their heads almost touched. Francis felt the heated stab of jealousy consume him.

A man of the church hurried out to meet them, his gestures indicating the gentle sorrow only men of God seemed so very adept at—being neither patronising nor false.

Lord, what if they were here to be married a few days after the old duke had gone to his grave and whilst still in mourning? Was that possible or even allowable? He was not certain of all the many and convoluted rules of the *ton*, but he did not imagine it could be thought of as remotely good form.

Another man had joined them and the group turned to mount the steps of the church, the older woman taking Sephora's hand on the other side and giving a perfect picture of familial harmony and solidarity.

Sephora Connaught looked small there between the larger-built Winburys as they all disappeared into the narthex of the church and then were gone.

'Hell.' He hated the fear in his voice and the feeling of hopelessness. He wanted to simply exit his own carriage and follow them up the steps to see what it was they were doing, to stop the wedding, if that was what was happening, to drag Sephora away and talk some sense into her, and say what?

Marry me instead?

Follow me into the dark corners of my life and understand my demons? He moved his head sideways and pulled on the stock at his throat. The ghost rope was there again. Too tight. He could not breathe.

Lifting his cane, he banged on the roof of the conveyance and was glad when it started to move, out into the row of traffic and away. These dreams were not for him. He had forfeited such luxury when he had shot Ralph Kennings from a distance. Three shots. All on target. The clouded eyes of death followed him even here amongst the mannered and gentle world of the *ton*, watchful and accusing.

He met Lady Sephora Connaught again the following week, this time at a small private gathering in Mayfair in Adam Stevenage's town house. The Winbury party was swathed in black though the sister, Maria Connaught, had managed to find an unusual shade of violet for her attire. A half mourning, Francis supposed, since she was not so intimately associated with the new duke.

Sephora looked the palest he had ever seen her, the whiteness of her countenance caught against the heavy dark of her clothes. Richard Allerly had his arm tied through hers and stood in his usual position at her shoulder, the newly acquired ducal title stamped into his bearing and authority.

Francis wondered why Winbury had deigned to come at all to such a small soirée, but Stevenage was wealthy and money talked, he supposed, to a man with grand and political aspirations.

Adam came over to meet him, a knowing smile on his face, and Francis's heart sank. If this was his way of getting him and Sephora Connaught together he'd done a poor job of it, his mind going over their last conversation at White's. If he had known that she was going to be here he wouldn't have come, but it was too late to simply turn tail and leave. When he'd looked at her left hand he'd seen that there was no ring at all on her third finger and a part of him had been more than relieved to find it thus.

'I hope you approve of my list of guests, Douglas. After your help the other week I thought I should return the favour.'

Francis could barely believe Stevenage to be serious, but as the host was called away from his side Richard Allerly turned to observe him. His greeting was cold.

'I had no idea you were a friend of Stevenage, Lord Douglas.'

'He is more of a recent acquaintance, Your Grace.'

Francis did not look at Sephora at all, but felt her there as her hand pulled away from Winbury's sleeve.

'If you will excuse me, Richard.' Her words were quiet and she left, threading her way across the room to stand with her sister. He was glad that she had gone.

'Lady Sephora and I are hoping to move our nuptials forward. My father's death…' Winbury stopped and for the first time Francis saw a glimpse of true emotion.

'I was sorry to hear of your loss.' It was the least he could say, this trite phrase, to fill an awkward social meeting.

'And I am sorry that we should have to cross paths like this, Douglas. I hoped I had made it clear in my letter that I did not want you anywhere near my wife-to-be ever again.'

'Well, Your Grace, if you had jumped into the damned river yourself I wouldn't have had to be closer to her in the first place.'

The gloves were off, though Francis moderated his tone given the social setting in which they stood.

'My bride's indebtedness to you is misplaced and foolish.' Now this was new. 'She does not know of the reputation you have garnered and she is a woman to whom wickedness and evil are unknown qualities.'

He almost laughed, but he didn't for the duke's tone had risen and all around people were stopping to watch. This was neither the time nor the place to instigate a conflict with the grief of a lost father so very present and with many ladies in the room.

'It has been interesting,' he replied and tipped his head before moving away. Lady Maria Connaught came to stand beside him a few seconds later as he was pouring himself a brandy.

'You probably like the duke as little as I do, my lord.'

'Pardon?' When he glanced up he saw Sephora Connaught watching them over her sister's shoulder. He also saw Winbury walking back to claim her, one arm again tucked through his as he drew her away.

'The Duke of Winbury thinks a husband should own his wife and direct her in all her actions and thoughts.'

'Unfortunate, then.'

At that the girl laughed, her dark eyes flashing. 'My sister is not happy. I think they would have parted company had the funeral not happened. As it is now Richard is using all his grief and sadness as a weapon. It is hard for Sephora to abandon such unhappiness, but I like to think she is just waiting for her chance of it.'

'Why are you telling me this?' he asked quietly, turning so that others might not come to encroach upon their conversation.

'Because you saved her once, my lord. Perhaps you might do so again?'

With that she left to rejoin her sister and when he caught the glance of Sephora Connaught upon him all he saw was fear and worry.

They had departed early, giving their apologies to Adam Stevenage and going home, Maria most upset to be leaving in such an unseemly rush.

'I would have liked to at least remain for the afternoon tea,' she grumbled as the horses wound their way into a row of heavy traffic.

'Then you should have had the good sense not to have conversed with Douglas quite so freely and you might have had that chance, Maria.'

'People are allowed to speak with whom they wish, Richard. This is England.'

Sephora's reprimand was sharp, she knew it, but the behaviour of her husband-to-be ever since sighting Francis St Cartmail had appalled and worried her. She didn't know what it was they had said to each other, but she had heard him raise his voice and knew Richard well enough to recognise his ire, an anger that continued to ferment even now, half an hour after the event.

'Douglas should be drummed out of the *ton*, for goodness sake, and would have been had he held a lesser title.'

'Mr Stevenage did imply the Earl of Douglas was almost as rich as he was. Perhaps that might be a part of the reason the *ton* does not shun him.' Maria said this calmly and Sephora took in her own breath before Richard could answer.

'It should not matter how much money he has,' she said, 'or what his title is. The Earl of Douglas saved me from certain death and for that I shall always be grateful.'

'Of course, my angel,' Richard muttered and took her hand.

'I do not particularly like that endearment, Richard,' she returned. 'It seems silly and inappropriate somehow for a woman of almost twenty-three.'

Her eyes met his, the dark anger in Richard's making her grit her teeth. She'd always humoured him and allowed him his way, but suddenly here in the carriage wending their way home she had had enough.

An ordinary Wednesday and a short and familiar journey. She could not truly understand what had just changed and broken between them, but it had, the two halves that had previously fitted together now beyond any point of reconciliation.

Smiling at the two sets of eyes turned towards her in surprise, Sephora simply stared out of the window and laid her hands in her lap, avoiding the action of wringing them together in concern.

She felt dislocated and scattered, seeing her life before her in no more than the space of seconds and minutes. Even hours seemed too far, too exhausting. She had no energy apart from the concentration needed to breathe into the next moment of her being.

She counted her breaths now often, because when things slipped out of control it gave her a small authority back, a will that was not being bent by others. Sometimes, though, she wondered if she might just slip into the space between reality and madness and never return.

Chapter Eight

Two evenings later Sephora sat and wrote another letter to the Earl of Douglas because she thought if she even left it for one more moment she would decide not to and by then it would be too late.

She asked Francis St Cartmail to meet her at Lackington's in Finsbury Square, in the back room behind the spiral staircase. That part of the Temple of the Muses was always deserted, housing most of the old and dusty treatises that were seldom lent out. Nobody would disturb them.

She set down a time and a place. The day after tomorrow at two o'clock in the afternoon. With all that had happened, she knew Mama would insist on a nap and she could use those hours to quietly escape. She had two books that needed returning and the library was one of the places she visited on a regular basis. No one would ask questions.

Of late, she had seen her mother watching her with a sort of veiled pity, the look one might give a wounded animal or a simple child. Once or twice Mama had even enquired whether she was happy with her betrothed, the questions phrased in a way that did not require any answer as she always added some anecdote of the material gains such a marriage would entail. New gowns. A beautiful house. A place in the *ton* that was almost unequalled. A title. Sephora, the new Duchess of Winbury.

In the past she had largely ignored these sorts of comments and got on with life. But now she found she couldn't. Richard was also pressing her for a wedding date and he wanted it to be a lot sooner than she had hoped for now that his father had passed away.

Without a great array of close girlfriends and with her sister away on a short holiday with their aunt, Sephora felt isolated and alone. Her life had stalled somehow into a shadowy place, the gloom of death, the sadness of grief, the inability of Richard to extricate himself from an ever-deepening hole of grief. The colour of black consumed her.

She was constantly fidgeting and was always scared—of saying something, of not saying anything, of waiting until a good time to break off untenable promises. She had got so worried by it all that she had come out into welts of hives, all over her arms and her back, the red and swollen itchiness making her irritable and impatient.

And right there and then, in the quiet of a late evening, Sephora felt exactly as she had when she had fallen from the bridge into the river all those weeks ago, breathless and cold, her world receding into darkness.

Suffocating.

This is what it felt like to die inside and yet still live. The realisation was so dreadful she could not even cry out.

She sat that way until the dawn when the first pink light of morning came and she knew, with every single part of her being, that she would die here if she stayed silent even for another hour.

It had been so long since she felt alive, so long since she had laughed or loved or lived. Properly. When she had seen Francis St Cartmail walk into the Stevenage town house the small flicker of something she'd thought dead inside her had been surprising. Vitality. Vigour. Desire. Pushing against all that was numb and frozen and telling her she could wait no longer. Picking up her letter, she ripped the sheet into a hundred pieces and hid them under other paper in her drawer. A letter would not do it. She would go and see him herself.

When her maid finally came to her room as the hall clock struck nine in the morning, she instructed the girl to find her navy day dress and her cloak and hat. Then with her hair put up and her cheeks rubbed into colour, Sephora simply walked down the stairs and out of the house before anyone at all would miss her.

Francis was coming from his library as the butler opened the door and he wondered who on earth would be calling in on the household at such an hour.

Lady Sephora Connaught stood there in a fine blue dress and cloak, a small purse in hand and her cheeks so pale, he thought she might simply fall over before he could reach her.

'Lord Douglas,' she said and then stopped,

taking a breath and beginning again. 'I need to speak with you privately, my lord, if you would be kind enough to allow me the time.'

'You are alone?' He took her arm and looked around. No one else was in sight. The sleeve of her cloak had fallen back and a large welt of redness was easily visible.

'Has somebody hurt you?' His heart began to thump as quickly as hers did, for he could feel the rapid beat of blood under his fingers.

'Pardon?'

'Your arm? Who did this to you?' When he pulled the sleeve up further there were more welts, barely a piece of skin unmarked.

She began to cry even as he looked at her, huge tears simply pooling in her pale eyes and falling down her cheeks.

'They…are…h-hives. I get…them when I am…scared.'

Swallowing down fury, Francis took her through to his library and shut the door. Just at that moment he cared nothing for propriety or the rule of manners. All he wanted to do was to take Sephora into his arms and hold her safe, but he made himself stand still. Why had she come here so early and so alone and why the hell was she so scared?

He made certain she sat in the most comfortable wing chair by the fire. It was cool this morning, the June temperatures diving after a warm spell. Bringing her a drink, he waited till she took a sip and then coughed.

'Wh-what is it?'

'Whisky. It fortifies the spirit.'

Carefully she took another sip and swallowed it. Her mouth puckered in distaste, but still she took a third.

'I need as much of…this as I can g-get, then.'

The fourth, fifth and sixth swallows had him leaning forward and taking the glass from her.

'It's usually not imbibed with such rapidity, especially if you aren't used to it, and it's a damn strong brew.'

She sat back at that, leaning her head against the leather and closing her eyes, the silence between them as perplexing as her appearance here. After a few moments though her glance caught his own and she smiled.

'You are very beautiful, Lord Douglas, but then I suppose many women tell you that. I am

a woman, after all, and I am telling you that.'
She hiccupped and her hand covered her mouth.

Hell. She was tiddly and fast becoming properly drunk. The whisky had been a poor idea.

'I cannot marry Richard Allerly, the Duke of
Winbury. I have come here to say this. To you.'

She was well in her cups and he should not
play the game that she had somehow started.
He should bundle her up right here and now,
ply her with strong coffee and have her taken
home before things got completely out of hand.
But he couldn't. The gentleman in him twisted
across desire and lust. 'Why do you not wish
to marry him?'

'Because…' She looked at him then with her
pale eyes, a hint of light grey at their edges. 'Because…only with you do I feel…safe.'

Safe? When all he could think of doing was
kissing her to feel again what he had in the
water, the warmth of her and the sweetness?
Safe—a sharp and innocent barb that both broke
his heart and firmed his resolve. He wasn't safe,
not by a long shot, but she couldn't know that
yet and he wouldn't tell her.

Stepping back, he took the blanket from the

sofa behind him, then wrapped it around her and brought her from the chair.

'Come, Sephora. I will take you home.'

He knew they had been observed leaving his town house, though he hoped the blanket might have obscured her identity from those who watched.

The ride back was quiet and quick, Sephora merely slumped against the seat opposite him, lost in thought. The Aldford town house had a small drive, an unusual but most useful amenity. He was glad to be free of the public gaze and yet the worst was probably to come.

A servant hurried down the stairs and opened the door and Francis helped Sephora out as she leaned on his arm, blinking her eyes as if she had trouble with her vision.

Her mother met them before they had gone three steps, the anger in her undeniable and immense and behind her the single figure of the Duke of Winbury hovered, his face as red as the welts on Sephora's arms.

'You!' There was no greeting and no explanation as he came forward, knocking Francis backward, and short of taking Sephora with him he simply let her go as he tumbled, leaving him no true time to protect himself, the hard edge of the marble steps connecting with his left temple and stunning him momentarily.

Then Winbury was kicking at his shoulder and his arm and his head. The day darkened, but he managed to get up, his own servant now between his assailant and him. Sephora's father, the Earl of Aldford, grabbed at the newly titled duke and slammed him up hard against a nearby wall.

'Stop.' Sephora's voice, from the bottom of the steps, panicked and desperate. 'Don't hurt him.'

Francis did not know whom she meant not to be hurt, but the blood from the gash at his temple was gushing down his face and he understood at that moment there was nothing to be gained by trying to explain. Not here. Not now. Not in the heat of argument and in the sharp pull of pain.

Lady Aldford was shouting, too, telling him to leave and never come back, Anne-Marie's name in the mix of her wrath. 'You have already ruined the life of my sister's daughter and I shall never allow you to despoil another.'

He felt oddly disconnected, the throb in his

temple worsening and his breath shortened. When his man took his arm he allowed him to lead him back to the waiting carriage, sitting on the seat with relief as the world spun in dizzying circles.

The last image he had of Sephora Connaught through the glass was of her turning towards the departing coach, and then falling carefully, quietly, down onto the sharp pebbled chips of the drive.

'Silly, silly girl.' Her mother's words echoed through the ache in her head and the dry pain of opening her eyes. 'Here, I have brought you hot milk.'

Lifting the beaker to her lips, Sephora was pleased for the warmth the drink provided as she scrambled for clarity. She was in her own bed and the day was darkening. Had she slept for all the hours in between? She remembered Francis St Cartmail plying her with a strong drink and him falling, his head cut and blood in his eyes. She remembered Richard kicking him, too, and her father trying to pull the duke away.

'I do not think he can forgive you for this, Sephora.'

'St Cartmail?' Her mouth felt dry and strange and her eyes could not adjust to the light.

'Not Douglas.' Decided anger now resided where worry had lingered. 'The Duke of Winbury, of course. You return from God knows where alone in the company of the dissolute and dangerous earl, drunk as any bosky in the land and expect your husband-to-be to simply shrug it off, disregard it? It is beyond the pale, Sephora, beyond any sort of reasonable excuse you could even muster. You shall be ruined. Forever.'

Her mother had begun to cry now, quietly, as she took back the drink and replaced it precisely in the middle of a cloth of folded white linen.

'You have never been a worry to us before. In all your entire life you have been a good, dutiful and sensible daughter, a girl who anyone might look at and think how very lucky we have been. Until the bridge. Until you fell off that bridge into the water below and changed completely.' Her sobs were louder now. 'Too many people saw you in St Cartmail's company and alone this morning. Richard had brought his aunt to visit us, a strident sort of woman of firm morals and unquestionable virtue. Circles, Sephora. Your behaviour is like throwing a pebble into a still pond, just a small disturbance at first and then an enormous one. We could smell whisky on your breath and you were barely coherent. I do not know how it is we will go on happily from here. In fact, I very much doubt that we can.'

'Papa?'

'Is heartbroken. He feels it is better if he does not see you just now.'

'And Richard?'

'Has gone. He sent a note to say how disappointed he was.'

Sephora turned away into her pillow, an anger surging. *Disappointed?* She knew exactly what that emotion felt like.

'I don't want to see him.'

'Well, Sephora,' her mother returned in a voice that had risen in both strength and conviction, 'I don't think that he wants to see you much either. But bear this in mind—if he does not wish to marry you, I doubt anyone else will want to either.'

Francis sat in his library with a sore head, a sore shoulder and a wrenched hand, but he sat neither alone nor at peace.

'I am telling you, Lord Douglas, the girl is a

wildcat and a hoyden and that never in all my years of being a governess have I come across the likes of this one.'

Mrs Celia Billinghurst was crying as she said this, tears leaking into the large handkerchief she held in one hand and the remains of a ripped book in the other. 'She takes no notice at all of anything I tell her. And today she…she simply disappeared from my side and did not return until a good forty minutes later. I thought she was dead.'

'Where is she now?' His jaw ached as he asked the question for the boot of Richard Allerly, the Duke of Winbury, had been remarkably accurate.

'Outside, sir. She has been told to sit and wait for me to call her.'

His heart sank. He would have to deal with the remains of another chaotic day in his household immediately on top of the fiasco at the Connaught town house. 'I shall see my cousin alone, Mrs Billinghurst, and let you know the outcome afterwards.'

'Certainly, sir. Though I will say that I need this job, my lord, and that I have excellent credentials as a governess and that you would be hard pushed to find another with such glowing recommendations.'

'Indeed.'

'But I do think the girl is hiding things, big things. I think she is scared of something in her past.'

'Thank you.' Francis waited until she had gone before pouring himself a stiff drink. He needed a moment before he saw his cousin and the last sight of Sephora Connaught as he had left the town house still worried him.

God, what had happened next? Had Winbury controlled his temper? Had her mother found hers? Had someone come and lifted Sephora inside to listen to her part of the story, to her concerns and worries and to understand the reason for her hives?

A small knock at the door had him turning and his cousin came through the door, her dark eyes worried and repentant.

Another girl who needed to be understood, he suddenly thought. Another young woman who had so far in her life been a pawn of all the adults surrounding her. He made himself smile as he asked her to sit.

'Mrs Billinghurst is finding your behaviour difficult, Anna.'

'I don't think she likes me much. I think she hoped I would be prettier.'

Now this was new.

'Why?'

'She said I needed different clothes and I needed to walk and talk different. She said my hair is all wrong and that my language was... dreadful.'

'And you don't wish to change?'

'Not all of that much. Perhaps a bit, but she wants it all different.'

'Should we start with your name, then? Would you like to be called Anna St Cartmail instead of Anna Sherborne from now on?'

'St Cartmail? The same name as yours, you mean?'

'As ours. You are a Douglas. It is only right that you should be called such and carry the name of the lineage you were born to.'

When she stayed silent Francis changed tack. 'Where did you go today? Mrs Billinghurst said that you were missing for forty minutes and she was worried.'

Anna coloured, but made no effort to answer him.

'Do you not like it here?'

That brought her eyes up to his. 'I do, sir. My room is nice and the food is good and I like the books.'

'But you ripped one up, I hear.'

'It was a baby book. Mrs Billinghurst said that I had to read it like a lady does.'

'A lady?'

'A lady who speaks like this.' She mouthed each vowel widely and he could not help but smile.

'What do you prefer to read?'

'Books on lands that are far from here. Stories of travel, biographies of people who have been places.'

'Such as who?'

'Jonathan Swift. Daniel Defoe. Lady Mary Wortley Montague.'

'Her letters from Turkey?'

Dark eyes sharpened. 'You have read them?'

The wife of the British ambassador had written of the Muslim Orient and Francis could not believe that this small and plain child might enjoy such a complex treatise.

'Come to my library tomorrow morning and I will show you some books I used to enjoy.'

'So I could read in my room alone?'

'Yes.'

She stood at that as if in tarrying he might change his mind.

'I would like to be known as Anna St Cartmail. I would like to be a Douglas like you.'

And with that she was gone, a slight and thin shadow against the walls, and if she had that look of the hunted at least she was starting to feel as if she might belong. He was pleased for it.

God. His day had gone from bad to worse and he did not know for once which way to turn. He wished Sephora Connaught could have been here to tell him what to do with a wayward and angry almost-twelve-year-old girl. That thought had him drinking the rest of his cognac in a quick swallow.

Everything about his life was skewered into wrongness and the 'angel of the *ton*' would hardly be interested in sharing such chaos. He was as damaged as Anna was, more so perhaps, and his household was falling to pieces around his ears.

He only hoped Sephora was safe and happy and that someone had taken her into their arms to reassure her that everything would all be right.

With a sigh he lifted his bell and asked Walsh to bring Celia Billinghurst to him. He'd need to tell the woman what had been decided for he wanted her to understand that Anna's place in his house was a right of birth and not of chance.

No cards came to ask the Connaught family to any social occasion, not the next day nor the one after that. Richard had neither called nor sent a note either and if a small part of Sephora was saddened by his actions, a much greater part of her felt only an enormous relief.

'Let's go out anyway, Sephora,' said Maria, who was now returned home. 'Let's walk for an hour or two. We don't have to speak with anybody at all.' Maria took her hand and pulled her from the seat she had been in for hours.

'I am not certain. This is all my fault and being seen with me in public will do your reputation no good. If I am to be banned from any social occasion forever, you still have the chance not to be and I think you ought to take it.'

Laughter was the only answer.

* * *

Half an hour later Sephora found herself on the pathway by the river, their ladies' maids trailing behind each of them closely.

'At least Mama has not come, Sephora, nor Aunt Susan. If there is something to be said about being a social pariah, it is that it at least allows one freedom.'

Sephora was not quite so certain as group after group passed them by without the shadow of recognition or friendliness. It was as if she did not exist any more and even people whom she might have imagined would be kind were not.

Finally they stopped and Sephora realised Maria had brought her to the exact spot where Lord Douglas had dragged her into the bank after her fall.

'Do you remember clinging on to the Earl of Douglas, Sephora? Clinging on with such a fervour Richard Allerly had to prise your fingers open to make you let go?'

'I do.'

'Do you remember, too, how Douglas shook with such ferocity his teeth chattered? A panic attack, I think, much like the one he had a few weeks ago at the Wesleys in the garden with you. He has dreadful secrets, Sephora. You can see that in his eyes even when he smiles. Adam Stevenage said that he was buried under a collapsed structure in a river once for hours in Georgia. Perhaps it was the mud here that made him remember. Did he shake in the same way out there in the deeper waters?'

He hadn't, she thought. He had held her to him with an iron grip as he kicked his way in, across the current, against the wind. But he had been steady and calm.

'Adam said that his cousin died in the same accident. St Cartmail was held at first for his murder. They nearly hanged him for it, but he was saved at the last moment.'

'By what?'

'The branch broke as he was in mid-air and the more superstitious amongst them took it as a sign from above for clemency so he was hauled into the local courthouse instead.'

Half-hanged? Sephora's eyes filled with tears. 'My God. What happened next?'

'The magistrate determined the bullet in Douglas's arm was the same as the one in the dead man and so he was proclaimed innocent as they concluded that someone else had fired the shots.'

The horror of it all had Sephora leaning against the trunk of a tree. Francis St Cartmail had been shot along with his friend? He had not told her anything of that. 'Is this common knowledge here, amongst society, I mean?'

'I am not sure. There are certainly many dark stories about him in circulation, but perhaps not that particular one.'

Why had she not heard of the gossip? Suddenly she knew. Because her life had always been sheltered and protected and Richard had had a big hand in that. Anything difficult or sad had been strained out and discarded, half-truths or no truth at all left in their place. The falsity of it all made her feel sick, for in effect she had been pushed to the side of life to live in a vacuum, all perfectly pleasant but no true and utter joy.

She could not help the tears that came as Maria put one arm around her shoulders.

'I think I have been asleep for years, Maria, like that princess in the fairy tale.'

'So take this as a gift, Sephora, for a near-death experience has woken you up.'

Unexpectedly they both laughed.

* * *

Richard arrived at three o'clock in the afternoon the next day at her bidding and he looked as if he had not slept for a week.

'Thank you for coming. I thought you might not.' Sephora had made sure that she was dressed today not in black but in her most sombre gown, a grey-and-navy silk over which she had laid a deep grey worsted wool shawl.

'Well, unlike you, I adhere to the manners and mores of our society and its proprieties.' He did not sound at all happy.

'I know you do.' Sephora had always realised this about him, but for the first time she only felt sorry for such compliance. 'I also realise I have put you into an awful position and would like to say that I quite understand if the terms of our betrothal are now untenable to you.'

'Untenable?' For a moment she saw the boy she had fallen in love with all those years ago under the sterner face of the man he had become. 'For whom?'

Not as easy as she had hoped, then. Resolutely she took in breath.

'We have changed, Richard, both of us. Once we knew who each other was, liked who each other was, but now…?' She spread out her hands. 'Now I think we would be better to remain as friends than as anything more.'

'No.' He grabbed her hand and brought it to his lips, the kiss he placed in her palm harsh and angry. Clenching her teeth together, she tried in vain to pull away.

There was nothing there. No passion or lust or joy. No want to take it further in the hope of more, just a deadness that was astonishing and a revulsion, too, if she were honest.

'It was the river, wasn't it? You changed after that.' He wiped his mouth with the back of his hand as he let her go, standing there breathing loudly. 'I should have jumped after you, but I didn't. Is it him? Is it St Cartmail that you want? He is a murderer and a liar and worse.'

She stopped him simply by turning away. 'No, it is because of me and you, Richard, and your father.'

'My father?'

'Uncle Jeffrey told me to find my life again that day you took me to see him. He said I had looked sad for a long while and I needed to find my passion.'

'Passion?' He laughed then and the sound was not kind. 'You have always been cold physically, Sephora, cold and distant. I doubt heartily that you could discover such a thing even if you tried.'

She let the insult pass as she drew into herself. He was hurt and striking out, though in his outburst she allowed him a kernel of truth.

'Then let me go. Let me break off our betrothal and allow both of us to be free again.' She could barely believe the words had come from her, strong words and certain. It had been so very long since she had felt such.

As if he had recognised the change he simply looked at her and stepped away. 'If I do as you ask, Sephora, you shall be looked at in pity. Society will crucify you. Believe me, you will regret this.' There were tears in his eyes and he wiped at his nose with a starched kerchief dragged from his pocket, but she could not allow the weak emotion of only pity to take away her newfound power of strength. It had to be all or nothing.

Reaching across to a low table, she rang the bell and a servant came into the room immediately.

'His Grace is just leaving.' She watched as Richard gathered in his temper and departed.

Chapter Nine

Francis spent the next five days in Hastings trying to piece together as best he could the movements of Anna and Clive across his final hours. He had procured the services of a man who worked for the Bow Street Runners and the meetings he had held in both Hastings and Rye were most illuminating.

It seemed Sherborne had dealt with a London lord in many of his drops of liquor, a man who signed his name simply with an artful and sweeping 'W'.

'Find this man and you will have your killer,' Alan Wilson said over a drink in a tavern just outside Rye. 'Sherborne was funnelling off both cash and kind and rumour on the ground has it he was found out. Nobody around these parts trusted him much, but they trusted the London cove even less. Besides, Clive Sherborne was seen with his daughter just prior to his murder by a woman who was late home and she said he gave the impression of being drunk and the little girl looked scared. Those about these parts said she was a hellion, too, undisciplined and ill bought up. End up like her mother she will, they told me, with her neck broken on the backstreets and her skirt up around her thighs.'

'Her mother was killed? When?'

'Two years ago this August.'

Hell, Francis thought, this sort of place was probably the environment Anna had spent most of her time in and yet still she could read and count better than most children of her age. Who had taught her? Could it have been Clive in his more lucid moments?

'Did you find out who lived in the house with them in Hastings?'

'An old scholar boarded with them. Timothy Hawkins. He died of old age a year ago now. The girl visited the grave often and left wild flowers.'

Another loss, then, in a life full of them. If Clive or her mother or his uncle had been in front of him now Francis might simply have screwed their heads off. Instead he finished his drink and worded his next question carefully.

'Could you go to London and follow the movements of two brothers and their father? I will give you their direction. It will need to be done discreetly, for I would like to know if they meet anyone who fits the description of a London gentleman.'

On his way back to London other matters settled into a cold knot in his stomach. He did not wish to see Sephora Connaught again after the fiasco at her family town house and he most certainly did not want to see her in society hanging on the arm of the Duke of Winbury. No news had filtered through of her wedding, however, and of that at least he was glad, but he needed space and time and distance to re-evaluate his life.

The morning after his arrival back at his town house he was surprised by an early visit from Daniel Wylde.

'You damn well need to do something about Sephora Connaught, Francis. She has been ostracised completely by every strata of fine society after breaking off her engagement and

Winbury has had a big hand in that by summarily dismissing her as a woman slightly deranged.'

This was the very last thing Francis had expected to hear and he remained mute in surprise.

'The Duke of Winbury is telling everybody that Lady Sephora Connaught has both an addled mind and a cold nature and that he is well shot of her. Your name was mentioned prominently as the main cause of her onset to a premature insanity.'

'Hell.' He turned towards the windows and opened them. 'I'd like to kill the bastard.'

'Well, you could do that, but a long stretch in goal will do nothing at all to help her. There are rumours swirling everywhere and one of the most persistent is that she came to visit you alone at your town house and that a number of people observed this reckless foray. It is also said that you packed her into your carriage and returned her home yourself when you knew there must be some repercussions from the unexpected visit.'

'It was the right thing to do. I thought a glass of whisky might fortify her, but she drank too much of it.'

Daniel laughed. 'Lord, Francis, you got her drunk as well? Then do the next right thing both for her and for you. She has been made an outcast. Adelaide said that she saw her and her sister out walking a few days ago and everybody gave Sephora the cut direct.'

'Hell.'

'You came home from America with the weight of the world on your shoulders and then you go right ahead and ruin the "angel of the *ton*."' Daniel breathed in heavily for a moment as though recollecting his thoughts and putting them into order. 'God knows what will happen next, but your own prospects for a satisfactory marriage have most likely just plummeted as well. A reasonable solution might be looking right at you.'

The last sentence made him ponder. Daniel had not been a man known to be overly interested in the marriage mart before and certainly had not tried to influence him on choosing a wife or a mistress if it came to that. 'Did Amethyst put you up to this?'

The slight hesitation told Francis that she had.

'My wife thinks you are lonely. She knows

there are things you are not telling us and she wants to help.'

'Tell her thank you for her worry, but also tell her that I am fine.'

'You might indeed be, but Sephora Connaught is far from it. What would make her throw her more normal caution and good sense to the wind and arrive at the home of a known and disreputable bachelor unaccompanied and unmindful of who saw her?'

Safety. He almost said the word, almost simply spoke it aloud and spat it out, but Daniel would understand that sentiment as little as he himself did and so he remained quiet.

'Well, I leave it in your hands, Francis, but I never took you for a man who would forsake a woman needing help and she is most certainly one who does.'

Two hours later Francis made his way to the Connaught family town house on the north side of Portman Square. A footman showed him in, his eyes widening as he realised just who the visitor was, and led him down a long corridor to the back of the house.

'Lord Douglas, sir.'

Aldford was sitting behind his desk in a well-stocked library and he got up as soon as the introduction was made.

'Thank you, Smithson. That will be all. Please see that we are not disturbed.'

'Very well, my lord.'

When the door closed silence filled the room for the moment it took for Sephora's father to gather his ire.

'I hope you have come here to explain and apologise, St Cartmail.' Jonathon Connaught's voice shook. He was only just holding on to a temper that reddened his face considerably. 'After the last time…' He stopped.

'Your daughter came to see me, Lord Aldford, and whilst it was true I should not have given her whisky to calm her down, I did not touch her either.'

'No, you brought her back home to ruination instead and then just left her to it.'

'I did not know that until today for I have been away from London this past week. I thought Winbury would have seen things right.'

The name seemed to make the older man even more furious. 'Don't talk to me about that coward,' he shouted. 'If his father knew how he had treated my daughter in her hour of need, he would be rolling around in his newly dug grave, I assure you. He has abandoned her completely.'

'I wish to marry her.'

'Pardon?'

'I have come today to ask permission for your daughter Sephora's hand in marriage, sir.'

The older man leaned against his desk heavily and sat down, reaching for a kerchief in an opened drawer, then running it across his brow.

'Why?' All the fight seemed to have gone from him.

'It is partly my fault she is in the position she now finds herself. I need to remedy that.'

'Remedy it. She barely knows you, St Cartmail. She probably even hates you. Her betrothal to the Duke of Winbury has been dissolved and a great measure of the problem is down to the fiasco you created. Did you know that?'

'I did not at first, but I do now.'

'So now you have the damn nerve to just walk in here and expect my blessings or my daughter's acceptance.' The ire had returned as fast as it had waned, but Francis had known this meeting was never going to be easy. 'From memory you are also the very same man who broke my niece's heart all those years ago and you did not even come to her funeral to pay your last respects. How could we trust you to actually do the right thing this time?'

Francis stayed silent, the faults of his past mounting against him.

'I can't think why you imagine either my daughter or I would agree to this proposal, Douglas.'

'If Sephora agrees to marry me, she will no longer be ruined. I can protect her.'

'Against everyone?'

'Yes.'

'And if she does not?'

'Then I will leave. I do not want further trouble. I will also promise my confidentiality in all that has been discussed today.'

'You swear by it?'

'I give you my word of honour.'

Frowning heavily Connaught called out and the same man who had showed Francis in before opened the door.

'Yes, sir.'

'Ask one of Lady Sephora's maids to summon her to the library, Smithson. I need to see her most urgently.'

* * *

Sephora was reading by the window in her room when one of the upstairs maids came bustling in.

'Lord Aldford requires your company in his library. He says it is important.'

'Very well.' Sephora laid down the book she was reading and smoothed out the creases in her muslin day dress as she stood. Papa seldom asked her to come to his library so formally. She wondered what had happened and hoped that there was not some new and difficult problem concerning Richard Allerly.

'Is the duke with him?'

'I don't believe so, Lady Sephora.' Relief at that answer blossomed.

'But he is not alone?'

'No, Lady Sephora. Smithson said there was a visitor.'

This produced a further worry. Stopping to take up her shawl from the chair, Sephora wrapped it around herself and followed the maid downstairs.

Francis saw the instant Sephora Connaught realised it was him because she blushed a bright red and faltered as she stepped into the room.

'Sit down, please.' Her father's voice was not gentle. When she was seated he began to speak again.

'The Earl of Douglas has come here today with a marriage proposal. A protection, he calls it. He wants you to be his wife because he knows the current predicament you find your-self in is largely of his own making and he needs to remedy it, a marriage to quell the howls of an offended *ton*, so to speak. As such he is proposing a union of convenience to mend broken reputations and to lighten the gossip of a dreadful scandal that shows no sign of fading away.'

Was her father a complete fool, Francis thought as he stepped forward.

'I am hoping you will do me the honour, Lady Sephora, of becoming my wife.'

'Of course she will not, Douglas. I cannot think of anything further from my daughter's mind than accepting your—'

Sephora stood and looked at him directly. 'Why would you ask this of me, Lord Douglas?' Her eyes were wide, the blue more noticeable today in her high emotion.

'Because he has ruined you, my dear. It's the very least as a gentleman that he can do.' Her father sounded at the end of his tether.

'You could hardly want this, my lord, to be tied in marriage so…inconveniently when everyone in society knows your poor opinion on the institution itself?'

Francis was about to reply when her father strode across between them and began to speak again.

'Douglas is renowned in the *ton* for being wild and dangerous and you would do well to remember that the Duke of Winbury, for all his faults, has not been said to have killed a man. It is you who should not want this union, Sephora, you who have been held in great esteem by the *ton* all of your adult life, yet are now the subject of ridicule and pity because of the poor choices you have recently made.'

Francis had heard enough. 'I am not quite without advantage, Lord Aldford. I have returned from the Americas with a great deal of wealth for one and the Douglas title is an old and venerated one.' He saw Sephora Connaught's knuckles were white where she held them twisted together, though the hives had gone, the skin to her elbow where her dress sleeves ended now unmarked and fair.

He could not begin to imagine a more awkward wedding proposal and was about to request some time alone to explain his reasoning, when rushing feet from outside put paid to such hopes. Sephora's mother bustled in, her eyes reddened and her face furious.

'The butler said that you were here, Lord Douglas.' She was looking straight at him. 'And I could not believe that you would have the nerve to be.'

'Elizabeth…' her husband began, but she did not let him finish.

'The man standing before us is the architect of all our problems, Jonathon, the sole reason we are in this conundrum and Sephora can no longer partake in anything at all in society—'

'St Cartmail has come to ask for our daughter's hand in marriage.'

That stopped her as nothing else would have and she looked at her offspring intently. Sephora was so much smaller than her mother and deathly pale. All Francis could see was worry stamped across her brow.

'What of Richard? What of him, Sephora? What of an understanding that should at least be given some weight due to its longevity?'

'I think Winbury may have cooked his goose,

Elizabeth, given his lack of any true concern for our daughter's plight. He has certainly been vocal in his criticisms of her.' Her father gave this damning summation of Winbury's character without as much emotion as before.

'He is grieving…'

'He is weak willed.'

'So you are saying…?' Sephora's mother's face had lost its flush and was now a ghostly white.

'Our duty, Elizabeth, is to see that our daughter is not ruined by gossip, and the earl, whilst the subject of much discussion, is also titled and wealthy in his own right. Believe me, it could have been far worse.'

A different silence settled now and Francis used the moment to push his own cause further.

'Might I have a moment alone with Lady Sephora?'

He thought her mother might refuse outright, but before she could speak, Sephora's father had taken his wife's hand and led her from the room. 'I will allow you two moments, Lord Douglas. Sephora, we will be right outside. If you need us, you only have to call.'

Then they were gone, with the seconds counting themselves down in the room.

Sephora spoke first. 'Thank you for asking for my hand in marriage, Lord Douglas, but of course there can be no question as to what my answer must be.' Her words were quietly said and she blushed again even as he looked at her and gave his own answer.

'I realise we barely know each other and there are things you do not understand about me, but society can be cruel in its dismissal of a reputation and yours has definitely suffered. If I am to have any hope of protecting you successfully, we would need to be married immediately, as soon as the banns are read. On a special licence.'

He was rushing her, but the sudden and shocking thought came that if he did not she would be persuaded to refuse him, so he kept going. He did not wish to be responsible for her demise. 'I would never hurt you, Sephora. At least believe that.'

She looked at him then, directly, the shock in her face obvious. 'A marriage of convenience would hurt us both, my lord. Usually they are not happy unions.'

Her solemnly given words were stated with the sort of honesty normally only employed by the minions of the church and he liked it. Liked her. Liked the soft truth and the gentle honour and her smile that was both shy and bold at the same time.

Everything she said was true and the thought that he could not possibly be serious in such a proposal came to the fore. He barely recognised himself as he stood there, for he was being beguiled by an innocent and one who would hold no knowledge at all of the sort of man he was. Sephora Connaught was a woman oblivious of the underbelly of society with its broken lives and empty promises; a place that was by far his most known milieu.

What the hell was he doing? Why the hell was she not turning tail and running as fast as she possibly could, her near miss with Winbury a potent warning to the agony she might well suffer with him? Why wasn't he? But she was speaking again in her soft voice, trying to understand who he was, what he was.

'I do have another question, my lord. Those people at Kew Gardens, the ones you were fighting, did they hurt you in some way to make you retaliate in that manner?'

'No.' He had to be honest. 'But I thought that they might.'

'I see.' The words were almost breathed out.

'I am not perfect, Sephora.'

'Perfection is a hard thing to live up to, I have found, my lord.'

'And there are many rumours about my past that are not all false…'

'I think I have heard most of them.'

At that he laughed. My God, he couldn't remember enjoying a conversation with a woman as much as he did with her.

'Your parents are not happy with my proposal. It is also something to consider. Your cousin, Anne Marie, fancied herself in love with me, but I hardly knew her and I certainly did not encourage her feelings or return them. I didn't attend the funeral because I was drunk. Not from unrequited love either, but from the sadness of it all. The futility of a young life suddenly gone.'

'Are you trying to put me off accepting you?'

'No.' The word came without thought. 'I'm not.'

'Then yes. Yes, I will marry you, Lord Douglas.'

Her parents were back in the next second, gliding through the door and taking up the space again between them and the strange dislocation that Francis felt was multiplied.

'Your daughter has agreed to become my wife so I'll have my lawyers call upon you to-morrow, Lord Aldford.'

'Tomorrow?' Her father's word was barely audible.

'I will procure a special licence in order to be married before the week's end. My lawyers will look at an agreement tomorrow afternoon and I would like your daughter present at the discussions.'

'An unseemly haste…' her mother began, but without further conversation Francis simply tipped his head to them all and took his leave, walking out into the daylight and down the steps to his waiting carriage, the sun today warming the skin at his neck.

The Earl of Douglas had looked furious and distant in all the time he stood there asking her to be his bride. Even when she had assented in private his expression had not changed, the scar on his damaged cheek underlining all that was unknown about him.

She did not understand him and he did not know her, yet she had agreed to marry him and with none of her usual timidity.

She should have refused and that would have been the end to it. He would have gone away with the knowledge that he had done the honourable and decent thing and she would have been left to get on with her own life.

But what sort of life would it be without him? That thought had her placing her hands across her mouth in terror. Could she accept a proposal of marriage that he couldn't possibly be happy with, a union based only on propriety and public expectation? It would never work, not in a million years, and they could both only be made bitter because of it. He'd said nothing of feelings, nothing of regard, nothing of anything save for his duty to see her reputation safe.

Sitting in her bedroom watching the moon through the glass, all Sephora could think of was the wedding night. She was almost twenty-three years old and the only man who had ever kissed her had been Richard, embraces that had been few and far between and hardly satisfactory. Besides which he had called her cold.

Whereas Francis St Cartmail...

She stopped and pulled her mind away from all she had heard of the earl's sexual prowess. He would hardly be happy when he realised the true state of her knowledge of the sensual arts. Oh, granted, there were men in society who relished the chance of instructing a virgin in the matrimonial bed, but the earl did not seem to fit into that category at all. He was too raw and too carnal.

'Carnal.' She rolled the word on her tongue.

He had asked her to marry him and she had said yes and if they did not know each at all she only had to think of Richard Allerly to understand the futility of years of congress. They had been friends forever and yet it was such a familiarity that had torn them apart and left them strangers.

Francis St Cartmail was unfamiliar, but he was also kind and every time she had been with him she felt safe and protected.

Could it be enough? Closing her eyes, Sephora put her fingers to her temples to massage the ache that was building there, a heavy, dull pain of confusion and anxiety.

Anna had locked herself in a cupboard when Francis returned home and Mrs Billinghurst was standing waiting for him so that she could relay the sorry saga of another day's chaos.

'She is impossible, my lord. We had just got

out of the carriage and suddenly she simply turned for home and when I got here she was in the wardrobe of her room and I have not been able to coax her out since.' Her young son was next to her and trying his hardest to give the distraught woman some comfort.

This was the first time Francis had seen the lad up close and as a worried visage gazed up at him he realised just how young he really was. Had he been schooled, he wondered, since his father's death? 'What is your name?' he asked the boy.

'Timothy.'

'How old are you?'

'I will be twelve next year, sir.'

A different worry now formed across Celia Billinghurst's face.

'He is a good boy, my lord, and is no trouble at all to anyone.'

'Does he read?'

'He began once...' Her voice petered out as she tried to deduce the reasons behind the question, but the lad stepped forward and answered.

'I do, Lord Douglas. I taught myself and I read whenever I can.'

'What do you read?'

'Old newspapers mainly, my lord. Once I

went to the library in Finsbury Square with my
father…' He stopped and swallowed.

'Did you like it?'

'I certainly did, sir.'

'Good.'

A few minutes later he stood in front of
the solid oaken wardrobe and knocked twice.
'Come out, Anna, I need to talk with you.'

There was the slide of wood and a click of a
lock and the door opened. His small cousin held
one of his books and a candle in her hand and
she had been crying.

This surprised him more than anything for
each time he had seen her she had been prickly,
angry and distant.

'Mrs Billinghurst said that you ran away from
her and came home here all by yourself. Why?'

'I don't enjoy shopping.' She lifted her chin
and faced him directly.

'Then perhaps you should stay home for a
time so that we will all know where you are. It
is dangerous for a young lady of your age to be
lost in a busy city for a great length of time.'

Relief crossed the small face. 'I can do that.'

There was something she was not telling him,
he was certain of it.

'Did you see someone in town whom you were frightened of?'

She shook her head, hard, the Douglas determination stamped into her eyes and, knowing such stubbornness would be hard to budge, he changed the subject.

'I would like to hire a tutor for you, Anna, and set up a small schoolroom here as an adjunct to your governess's lessons for I think your mind is a lively one and could do with further training. Mrs Billinghurst's son, Timothy, is about your age and he enjoys reading as much as you do. How would you feel about having a fellow student in your class for two days a week?'

'I would like that.'

'Good. Then you now need to go and find Mrs Billinghurst and apologise to her. We can discuss further arrangements tomorrow when we are all feeling less emotional. Oh, and, Anna, I would prefer it if you called me Uncle Francis. We are family and it is only right.'

Much later that evening as the clock struck the hour of two Francis sat by an opened window in his library with a heavy woollen cloak about him to keep out the cold. He never slept well and tonight after all the happenings of the day he knew he would sleep even worse than usual.

He wondered what Sephora Connaught was doing. After leaving the Aldfords' town house he had gone straight into Doctors' Commons and begun the proceedings for a special licence. Could they be married the day after tomorrow with such unseemly haste and with so little pomp and circumstance?

They would need separate bedrooms, of course, with his poor sleeping habits and their lack of knowing each other at all, but he hoped in time…

What did he hope?

He hoped that she might begin to see him as he had been once before his stay in Hutton's Landing, before his life had been shaped differently, before he had killed a man in cold blood and not just under the protecting banner of war.

He'd never had a family, never had anyone who had lived with him for a very long time. His uncle and aunt had tried to be some sort of guardians to him, he would give them that, but he had been rebellious and angry after the early death of his parents and when he'd barely let them in, they had not endeavoured for a closer acquaintance.

School had fostered his friendships with Daniel and Lucien and then later Gabriel. And now Anna had come and Mrs Billinghurst and the son who looked frightened and intense and needy. A house filled with problems, but also with life. He could feel them all here around him and despite the quandary he liked the new energy.

Tipping his head, he took in air once and then twice more. He could barely believe Sephora Connaught had agreed to marry him and hoped that she would not hate him when she knew him better.

A dog barked in the distance, plaintive and sad, and the sound rolled around with that particular nuance of hopelessness he himself had often felt. A homeless animal, probably a stray. If the thing came closer, he would instruct his kitchen staff to go out and take it a bone.

Chapter Ten

Sephora fussed around and could barely settle all of the next morning because she knew Francis St Cartmail would be here in the afternoon with his lawyer. Would he have changed his mind? Would things today look very different from what they had yesterday as he realised the extent of what he had promised and regret it? Would he simply take his troths back and leave her here, the ruin of her name too daunting even for him to try to manage?

When he did finally come she thought he looked tired, the shadows beneath his eyes darker today than she had ever seen them before.

'Douglas.' Her father's greeting was cold, but

when the earl's glance found her own he smiled and she forgot everything else entirely.

'Lady Sephora.' Her name slipped from his tongue. 'I hope I find you well this afternoon.'

'Indeed you do, my lord.' With Papa and both lawyers present she did not dare to address him less formally though she would have liked to, given the circumstances. It was not normal, she knew, for a woman to be present in such discussions of money and law, but as Francis St Cartmail had expressly requested her presence her father under duress had allowed it.

'I have procured a special licence,' the Earl of Douglas was saying now. 'We can be married tomorrow for my lawyer is here to set the terms.'

'Tomorrow?' Was it even possible to marry legally in so short a frame of days? She could not stop her interjection.

'If that is what you wish?' He suddenly looked more uncertain and his eyes went to the windows.

'It is, my lord.'

'You cannot mean this, Sephora.' Her father spoke now. 'You have no dress, no invitations sent, no plan for a chapel or music or the food.'

'I do not need those things, Papa.' She said

this as she looked straight at Francis St Cartmail and saw the stiffness in him relax. He was trying his hardest to see her safe. The least she could do was to allay his fears of her own hope of a much larger celebration.

'Your mother will be even more horrified than she is now.'

Again the Earl of Douglas looked at her. 'If it is a grander ceremony you wish for…'

'I don't.'

His hand pushed his hair back from where the darkness had fallen over his forehead and he breathed hard. He always wore his neckcloth tied high and often pulled at it with his fingers, Sephora thought. The 'half-hanged' explanation of Maria's came back to her and she looked away. What sort of mark would a rope leave, both inside and out?

For a moment she imagined Francis St Cartmail naked under candlelight on their wedding night; this thought so unlike anything she had ever had before she almost blushed. In all of the years she had known Richard she had not once thought of him in any sort of a sexual way and she understood with a stinging clarity why she had not.

He had not intrigued her as Francis St Cartmail did, just one glance from his hazel eyes sending her into fantasy and folly. Richard had been staid and dictatorial and set in his ways and she had gone along with every single one of his orders and protocols. For years.

'Well then, what is it you are proposing in financial terms, Lord Douglas? My lawyer is most interested to know.' Her father was a man who thought the bottom line singularly important. She waited for the earl's answer.

'All that is mine shall be my wife's on marriage, save for the entailed Douglas properties as these will be passed on directly to any heirs. Any profit from the manufacturing businesses shall also be hers.'

Heirs? A short burst of heat had her reaching for the nearby back of a chair.

'That is indeed generous, my lord.' The Connaught lawyer opened his folder and wrote down the pledge. 'You speak of your garment interests, I am supposing?'

'He does.' The Douglas lawyer brought his files forward now and her father joined them, comparing notes.

When Francis St Cartmail caught her eye and

smiled, she imagined he could see the pulse in her throat leaping to his attention and turned back to her father.

'There will be a dowry, of course,' he was saying, 'Amongst other monies and properties settled upon her, my daughter owns an estate in the north that her grandmother bequeathed her and it is both fertile and in good order.'

'Lady Sephora can keep that for herself. I do not wish the gift to pass into our communal property.' The words of her husband-to-be astonished her.

'But…' his lawyer began, and the earl silenced him with only a look.

Hers. Brockton Manor was to be only hers? The hope of it made the day brighter and her mind surer. A generous husband and a fair one. Richard Allerly was wealthy, too, but she could not have imagined him passing up the offer of another estate. He liked things under his control and his say so.

Her father was looking at St Cartmail now in a way he had not been half an hour ago, the Connaught legal representative writing his concessions down as fast as he could, his pro-

fessional demeanour honed in for the best of
advantages.

Finally a draft of the marriage agreements
was signed. The Earl of Douglas's signature was
bold and he was left-handed. His middle names
were Andrew and Rothurst. So many things she
did not know about him. The large cabochon
ruby in his ring twinkled in the light and for
that familiarity she was glad.

Her father crossed the room and extracted
an expensive bottle of red wine when they had
finished, a tipple he rarely opened because of
the cost. The butler laid out five glasses, but
Sephora merely played with hers, the thoughts
in her head spinning. Lord Douglas was wealthy
and he was generous. He was also a force to
be reckoned with in the gaining of an equitable marriage contract that was suitable to them
both. All afternoon he had been certain to in-
clude her in every decision and had taken into
account her opinion concerning the points she
wished to comment on.

The meeting broke up then and after a quick
and formal goodbye the man she would marry
tomorrow at one in the afternoon at the chapel
of St Mary's was gone.

Her father finished both his glass of wine and hers. 'Waste not want not, though at least St Cartmail was easier to deal with than Winbury,' he said when he had finished the second. 'In my mind Douglas is either a saint or a fool with his capitulations of money and business interests and time undoubtedly will tell us which of the two it shall be. For your sake, Sephora, I sincerely hope that it shall be the first.'

Maria arrived home just on dusk and Sephora was glad to hear footsteps running up the stairs, her door bursting open even as her sister was undoing the bows on her bonnet.

'I cannot believe so much has happened, Sephora. In the two days I have been helping Rachel Attwood with the arrival of her new baby Richard is finally gone for good and in his stead is the Earl of Douglas? Even in my wildest dreams I did not imagine such luck.'

They came together in the middle of the room, Maria cold from the short carriage ride across the city and Sephora warm from the fire, their arms wrapped about one another as if they might never let go.

* * *

'I think Francis St Cartmail offered to marry me out of guilt,' Sephora said an hour later, after the whole story had been relayed in each and every minute detail.

Her sister shook her head. 'Society has been gossiping about the earl for years now. Do you really think a man like that could be brought to heel by Richard's meanness or by Papa's anger? Have you spoken with him, privately, and asked him why he should offer you marriage?'

'I have not had the chance. He came yesterday to relate his intentions to Papa and today with his lawyers to make it official. The two moments Father did allow us to converse alone were largely taken up with him saying that he would never hurt me and with me unable to say a word that made any sense.'

'Do you love him?'

Sephora drew her nightgown up around her neck, feeling a sudden chill in the room. 'I don't know what love is. I thought I loved Richard once, but…' She trailed off before trying again. 'Francis St Cartmail makes me feel…safe.'

'Safe enough to take risks? Safe enough to

be yourself? Safe enough to imagine that your opinion matters again?'

'Yes.'

Maria began to laugh heartily and fell back against the pillows at the head of Sephora's bed. 'I go away and come back to find my sister has defied all the convoluted and restrictive social mores that she has always adhered to and has absolutely no qualms or remorse for any of it. Mama is in bed with her smelling salts, Papa is counting the financial largesse of this new suitor and the *ton* is still talking of nothing else save the fall from grace of its most stellar and malleable angel. I think I should go and see my friend more often, Sephora, I really do.'

'Will you stand up with me tomorrow at the ceremony?'

'Tomorrow? My God. You cannot be getting married tomorrow?'

'By a special licence. I am wearing my blue silk, the one I had made for the Cresswell ball earlier in the Season, but did not go because I fell ill.' Her most striking dress was heavily embroidered with silver lamé and embellished with Brussels lace. Flowers and shells in the same silver threads festooned the hem, the whole thing having the effect of catching the light in a most unusual manner.

Sephora wondered how she could even think about something as unimportant as the colour and detail of her wedding gown, but unless she concentrated on the small and basic things under her control she thought indeed she might go to pieces. Would Francis St Cartmail insist on a marriage night before they had barely conversed? Or might he simply take her to his family seat in Kent and leave her there, a bride he did not want, a woman who had stumbled into her own marriage through a series of foolish mistakes? An inconvenient bride.

It was not truly his fault all this—it was hers. It was she who had gone to see the Earl of Douglas in the daylight and in an unwise lather of hope and hopelessness. He had not poured the whisky down her throat either; in fact, he had tried to stop her from drinking too much after offering it as a way to lessen the shaking in the first place.

Was he sitting there now in his town house not two miles from here rueing the day he had ever jumped from the bridge into the waters of the Thames to try to save her, and was her sister's romantic slant on the forthcoming nuptials as naive as her own imaginings of safety?

Sephora shook her head. The one thing she was very certain of at least was that she had made a lucky escape from the overbearing ways of the Duke of Winbury. For that at least she would be eternally grateful.

She was dressed in blue and silver and held a small posy of gardenias and green leaves. Her hives were back, too, he noticed, the fiery red marks crawling up the exposed skin on her lower arm and along the slender plane of her neck before dipping into the high-cut bodice at the front, a small fair figure, diminutive and pale against the other three members of her family who had accompanied her.

Lucien stood as best man, a last-minute favour when Francis's intent of doing this completely alone had wavered and he had asked for some assistance. This wasn't how Francis had imagined his wedding day might be, a hastily thrown-together affair with a bride who looked like she might simply faint away if he touched her.

'Your intended does not appear exactly happy.'

It was true. The woman who had said yes to

him was now enveloped in a sort of fog of distance and a state of fear, as if just by the blink of an eye this whole charade might simply disappear, her life back to the ordained and gentle path it had been sailing along less than a week ago.

There were no other wedding guests either and the minister was observing each small separate party with a look of concern and worry. At least there was someone playing the organ in an upper-storey loft, for the music covered the awkward quietness and offered a vague tone of religious fervour.

'Do you have a ring?'

'Yes.' Francis fumbled in his pocket for the small box and handed it over. Lucien flipped the top.

'Substantial.'

His friend's surprise seemed to give some sort of signal to the minister and he called them together, the age-old words of the Anglican marriage ceremony ringing out as an echo in the emptiness of the church.

'The grace of our lord Jesus Christ, the love of God and the...'

Francis moved to position himself next to

Sephora Connaught. He could smell the scent of the flowers she held and this close up he saw she shook quite badly, all her attention on the minister who had raised his hands in a welcome.

The sister was watching him closely, however, her dark eyes running across his own in a frank appraisal. Maria Connaught, unlike Sephora, did not look like a young woman who would be cowed by anything. He wondered about the difference between them. What made one sister brave and the other frightened, one woman ready to fight and another to flee?

As if on their own accord Sephora's eyes lifted to his and he saw inside the fright a further sense of resolve. Without thought he reached for her hand and her fingers curled into his own and held on. Like two people drowning together.

The oaths and promises were lengthy, but finally the rings were exchanged. His grandmother's diamond-and-ruby circle fitted Sephora perfectly, the fragile stones setting off the shape of her hand, an ancient and unusual piece that would never be repeated anywhere.

It was over just as she thought it might never be, the onerous frown of the minister, the still silence of Francis St Cartmail, the quiet weeping of her mother and the stony face of Papa.

'You may kiss your bride now.'

But he did not. Rather the Earl of Douglas's thumb simply ran down across one cheek before he turned away, breaking any contact with her and speaking to Lucien Howard next to him.

'Will you journey down to Kent today?' The Earl of Ross asked her this question a few moments later as they moved from the church and climbed inside the waiting carriages ready to take them home to the Aldford town house in Portman Square and the prepared wedding breakfast.

'Is that where the rest of his family are, my lord?' She wondered why no one had come to stand with him. Surely there must have been some relative who would have sufficed?

The earl shook his head. 'Francis's friends have that honour, for his own parents were gone when he was ten. I should probably leave it to him to tell you his story, though, but what I will say is that he has been lonely.'

Lonely. She could see that sometimes in his eyes and in the way he watched others, a careful isolation and a remoteness that allowed few near. She wanted to make him smile, she did, even just to see the ruined dimple on his cheek crease into laughter.

As though he could read her thoughts he turned, a half-smile making him look more vulnerable and younger, his eyes an unfathomable and mixed shade of green and brown.

'It won't be long before this is all over.'

Did he wish for it to be? Had he had enough of the enforced joyousness and the false congratulations? Her mother was still weeping and had given her nothing of maternal advice at all. Maria seemed to be the only one enjoying the occasion.

'I shall be married in exactly the same manner—' her sister's voice was light and happy '—without fuss of pomp and ceremony. And afterwards I shall journey to Italy on a grand tour with my husband and stay in the hot climes for a year and a day.'

Half an hour later the party was seated in the Aldford dining room and food was being served, numerous and special plates presented with artistry and attention. But Sephora could barely eat because soon it would be just her and

Francis St Cartmail, with all the corners of her shadows visible. Then Lord Douglas would discover what he did not now know.

She lacked gumption and adventure and interestingness, and for a lord who had sailed oceans and stood on foreign shores, faced danger and survived numerous threats, that might well be the most damning truth of them all.

When he stood to raise his glass and make a toast she wondered what he might say of her, a bride he'd hardly conversed with, and barely touched. The room became quiet and as he began to speak he turned towards her parents.

'First I would like to offer my gratitude to Lord and Lady Aldford for all the love they have given to their daughter. It is undoubtedly this attention that has made Sephora into the woman she is today. Thank you for allowing me her hand in marriage and I promise I shall give her the same care as you have. Always.'

Her mother had placed her kerchief down now and was tentatively smiling. Her father gave him an answering nod and finished yet another glass of wine.

'Sephora and I met unexpectedly, under the waters of the Thames, and I suppose that first encounter set the tone for our courtship. It has been a quick and breathless liaison.'

He waited till the laughter stopped and raised his glass.

'To my bride and to our marriage.'

She was glad Francis had not dredged out words of love because they would have been as false as Richard's constant proclamations of the same. Her fingernails left crescent marks in the soft skin of each opposite palm with the stress of worry and nerves.

After the toast Lucien Howard stood up as the best man.

'Francis has always made his mind up quickly. He has lived life to the full, though there are many stories of his exploits that have taken on a falsity all of their own. I have been a friend of the Earl of Douglas for a long time and he is one of the most honourable and virtuous men I know. After losing his own parents early he has become the man he is without the guidance of any family whatsoever.'

Her groom looked as if he wished Lucien Howard might cease altogether with the compliments. But he didn't as he turned to look at her. 'He saved me once, Lady Sephora, almost in the same way as he saved you. I'd dived into the high dam at Linden Park and got caught in the weeds and it was only Douglas's quick thinking that got me up to the surface before I ran out of air completely. So here's to happiness and to a long union,' he added and raised his glass.

Virtuous and honourable. Those were the words the Earl of Ross had used and she believed him, a man who would know Francis as well as any. The wine was sweet and easy to drink and it put a buffer between this moment and the wedding night, though the hives she had woken with were becoming larger and larger red welts of itchiness.

Her mother looked somewhat happier and her sister was glowing and if her papa was drinking far more than he ought then still her family had behaved. They had got through such a charade with a sense of grace. Sephora was eminently glad for that.

An hour later she rearranged her skirt and allowed her new husband to see her into the carriage, her parents and her sister standing on the pavement waving goodbye. Then they were alone, the busy streets of London town all around them, a procession of people and carriages and noise.

Her carefully packed luggage was in the back, an array of new clothes inside, a nightgown and a peignoir made of the softest apricot silk and edged in Brussels lace. Her mother's gift that, procured yesterday from one of the most expensive French seamstresses in the city, so new it was still wrapped in the tissue it had been bought in.

'We will go back to my town house first and collect a few things, but we will need to be on the road to Kent before mid-afternoon as I don't want to be too late in arriving.'

Too late? For what? Sephora thought. For a night alone? For more whisky, but this time plied for the very purpose of softening resistance? He had let it be known that there would only be a few servants accompanying them to Colmeade House, a private affair then, with all the hours of solitude. The Earl of Douglas sat on the same side of the conveyance as she did, but he had made sure to leave a large gap between them. Nothing touching.

A stranger and one who did not try to break the silence with other talk. The beautiful ring he had given her caught at a thread on her gown and snagged it. She spent a moment trying to tease the fabric away from the pointed sharpness of ancient gold and saw that it had left a hole in the silk. Like her life, broken, no matter how hard she might try to fix it and a sign of all that might come?

'It was my grandmother's,' he said unexpectedly. 'The ring. My mother gave it to me a few months before she died.'

'How did she die?'

'A carriage accident. My father was with her. I was ten at the time.'

'So afterwards there was no one else left for you? Today in the chapel…' She thought of the empty space on his side of the pews. 'Lucien Howard told me at the church that he and his friends were as much of a family to you as any and yet they were not there either.'

He leaned over and took her hand, his fingers as cold as her own.

'Daniel Wylde and Gabriel Hughes are out of London and I hadn't the time to wait for them to return. I'd spend a lot of weeks with them in the school holidays because it was lonely at the Douglas seat and the servants needed a break.

One small child could have hardly warranted the full opening of a large house after all and I was glad to go to where there was some sense of family and laughter.'

'Who were your guardians, then?'

'My uncle and his wife, but they were dour and busy people who were not much bothered with my needs. They hadn't their own children, you see…'

'So you were alone?'

He smiled. 'I suppose that I was. I don't think I've ever told anyone as much about my upbringing as I have you and if you'd…'

He faltered suddenly, his face changing from repose to complete and utter astonishment as he looked out the window, his cane snatched up from beside him and heavily brought against the ceiling.

'Stop, right now.'

The conveyance skidded to a halt and her new husband was out of the door, a knife in hand procured from beneath the seat, its shining honed blade caught in the sunshine as he moved.

'Stay here.'

But Sephora had already left her seat and was behind him, pushing into the path of the traffic, rushing through in the small spaces left between the busyness and pulling in her skirts close so that she could indeed run to keep up.

Ahead a small girl was being dragged along by a man who had her pinned to him by one arm and she was screaming her head off whilst trying to kick back. A wicked punch across the jaw silenced her, but the rage that erupted from the earl at the action brought every face from yards around towards him.

After that things began to happen in slow motion as Francis St Cartmail slashed out with his knife and the offenders gave answering jabs with their own weapons. Two other men had joined in the fracas now, with their anger and fury. One went down, a gash across his thigh opening into red, but the gun that the third offender held was primed and ready and it discharged point blank into the shoulder of the Earl of Douglas. He fell slowly, grabbing the child and using his momentum to roll with her, the shouts of bystanders, the frightened sobbing of the girl, the whitened clammy face of her new husband as he came to a stop by her feet and lay still upon the dirty camber of the road, panting.

The man with the gun moved forward to try

to extricate the child from his grasp, but Sephora simply fell on top of them both in protection, her generous silken skirts wrapped around everything as the warm seep of red blood darkened the thin fabric.

And she screamed, too, as loud as she could and as long, bringing bystanders to her aid even as she hung on to the small shaking body of the child with all the strength that she could muster and felt a hefty kick into the exposed fleshy part of her lower back as an angry retaliation for her efforts.

Then their attackers were gone, carrying the other man Francis had wounded between them and leaving a dozen or so spectators gathering about the ensuing brokenness that was left, not quite knowing what to do.

'Help. Please.' She could only mouth the words, her breath lost in the vicious last stab of pain and the horror of violence so unexpectedly meted out.

The child between them was sobbing so hard that Sephora had to gather her own will, the young girl demanding attention and some semblance of safety from the adults around her. The earl was still largely conscious at least, his hands held out before him stiff with blood and a clammy sheen of sweat across his face.

'Anna?' He looked about blindly. 'Is…she… safe?'

'Here. She is here.' Presuming Francis must mean the child, she wrapped the girl against her warmth and saw what she had not noticed before. The same hazel eyes. The same lines of beauty. The same colour of hair and grace of movement. The same stubborn line of jaw.

His daughter? His offspring? Just another secret that he had allowed her no knowledge of?

All her marriage lines fell into a dissolving welter of lies and omissions though her attention was caught by his raspy laboured breathing as he fumbled to loosen the stock at his neck.

When the white linen fell away she knew another truth as well. The deep red twisted line of where a rope had cut into his flesh was easily visible, knotted welts of skin raised one over the other, and a shocking hue of indigo beneath.

Hurt. Damaged. Left for dead. Once before and now yet again.

She lifted his head carefully, the matted dark curls falling dank across her fingers, and then she pressed her hands down hard against the welling bloodied hole in his shoulder.

'Get a doctor,' she shouted and refused to let him pass into the care of anyone else until a proper physician had come.

The first hours afterwards had been the worst.

Once home at the Douglas town house and upstairs in his chamber, Francis had begun to breathe in a strange way, blood gushing from the hole just above his shoulder blade.

'Elevate him,' the Douglas physician had instructed and with the help of a few of the servants they got him off the bed and sitting up in a large chair nearby.

Sephora was panicking, but Francis wasn't. He simply sat there gathering in his hurt and his circumstances and moderating his breathing as best he could. The bandage the doctor tightened around him finally allowed the blood to congeal, but would no doubt gush again with any movement whatsoever.

The earl's eyes were closed, the dark bruising beneath them worrying, and he was clammy. Shock, perhaps. Sephora found a heavy wool blanket at the foot of the bed and draped it across him as Mrs Wilson bustled in with a young servant and instructed her to light the fire.

'I do not think the bullet has injured any organ of great import.' The physician lifted up his bag as he said this. 'But it is a nasty wound and will need to be tended with great care in order to stop fever or inflammation from appearing. There is also a severe gunpowder burn around the site that will be painful so I will leave medicine to be administered and return on the morrow. The instructions are on the label, but the thing needed most now is a good dollop of sleep so that healing can begin to take place.'

The child, his daughter, had sat next to Sephora without speaking for all of the last hour, refusing to leave the side of the earl. Up close she looked older than Sephora had first thought her and much more unkempt. Her eyes were large orbs of pure and utter fright and her hands were freezing as Sephora brought the girl into her side, trying to warm her.

As her initial stiffness relaxed Sephora felt thin cold arms creeping about her middle.

'It is quite, quite all right, Anna,' she said

softly, remembering the name the earl had used. 'The earl will recover, I am sure of it, and this terrible fright will be a thing of the past…' She stopped even as she said the words, recalling her own dislocation after her fall from the bridge. 'You are safe now. Nothing will ever happen like this again. You will always be safe.'

The shaky nod almost broke her heart, a child trying desperately to find her courage and appear brave, but when Mrs Wilson reached out and told the girl to come away Sephora could do nothing but watch her go.

'I hope she is not too hurt. The man who tried to take her on the street hit her across the mouth…'

She did not quite finish as the housekeeper nodded. 'Anna disappeared from the side of her governess earlier in the afternoon and could not be found. Mrs Billinghurst was most upset.' Her voice petered out as the physician stood to leave.

'We will put his lordship into bed now with pillows to prop him up. He needs sleep to regather his energy.' Three manservants carefully lifted him off the chair and across to the bed where the covers had been pulled back so that he could simply slip inside.

He groaned at the movements and breathed in a rough manner, but once there appeared more comfortable, the blood from a cut on his right hand staining the snowy white coverlet. So much blood, she thought, glad that the Douglas physician had not wanted to bleed him further. His pallor now was as pale as the sheets of the bed he lay in and his breath was shallow.

Another few moments of flurried activity and then everyone was gone with only silence left as Sephora shut her eyes and held her head in her hands. Today had been a revelation. Francis St Cartmail had a child, a girl child, and she looked neither much cared for nor particularly happy.

The horror of it struck her anew. What sort of man could be so lax with the needs of a daughter? Her hair stuck out in all directions, her nails were as dirty as her clothes and he had not even asked her to his own wedding?

She struggled to find some sense in the whole thing. He had gone to save the child without thought for himself and nearly died for it. Surely that must count for something and the girl had stuck like glue to his side in all of the doctoring and aftermath. Her behaviour was not exactly that of a well-raised daughter and the manner in which she had sworn roundly as they had lain in a heap on the side of the road was most surprising.

Mrs Wilson had appeared wary of the girl, as had the servants. A child who might lash out, Sephora thought, or refuse any direction? An uncivilised and worrisome child.

Her own head had begun to ache with the direction her thoughts were going in. Francis St Cartmail had wed her today without mentioning that he had been married before and had heirs already. What of the legal documents and the implications for an heir already existing? My goodness, the scandal that followed him had arrived with a hiss and a roar on her very doorstep and not two hours after they had been wed.

'I am not perfect.' She remembered his words. But there was long distance between the lies and deceit she was suddenly confronted with and the small discrepancies she was imagining.

A marriage of convenience. A marriage forced upon him. A marriage that had not even begun before it was threatened.

She swiped at the tears that fell across her cheeks and sat up straighter. She would not cry. She was beyond even allowing such a release.

She would wait for the Earl of Douglas to regain consciousness and then she would find out exactly what else he had not told her.

It was late when Francis awoke, a single candle burning on the side table in his room at the Douglas town house in London.

This was wrong.

He should be somewhere else. There was a substantial pain across his shoulder and the smell of stale sickness in the air. He wore nothing but a sheet draped over him, and he began to gingerly move pieces of his body to see what functioned still and what did not.

Sephora. The name made him take in his breath and hold it, the ache of hurt radiating downwards in a sharp and jabbing violence.

'You are awake?' Her voice was soft in the late-night silence and he looked around. His new wife sat on his other side dressed in different clothes than she had last been in, her hair tied back in a simple knot, small golden curls escaping such confinement on each side of her face. There were deep shadows under her eyes and a bruise across her cheek that had not been there before.

'What happened?'

'You were shot, do you remember?'

He nodded, the noise and the instant pain coming back.

'Anna?'

'Your daughter is safe.'

He shook his head. God. He'd not managed to safeguard either of them, but had gone down with only the barest of resistance. 'Make sure… they…don't come back.'

It was all he could do, give such a warning before the dark and pain returned and he was once again floating.

The next time he came awake there was sunlight at the windows and he was glad that it was not night. He felt better, less light-headed. He was also very thirsty.

'Is there something to drink?'

Sephora was there again, soft and competent, her hands raising his head so that he could take a sip of some lemon concoction and just as gently lowering it down again.

'How long…have I been here?'

'Two days. For the first day the doctor thought you might not live and when you took fever he was certain of it. But you pulled through and now he is pleased with your progress.'

'And Anna?'

'I have not seen her again, though I hear her, of course. Your daughter is remarkably unruly.'

'She is…not my…daughter. I am her guardian and she has only recently come…to me.'

Sephora looked away from him, her blue eyes filled with pain and a hint of relief.

'No one explained this to me.'

'She is my uncle's illegitimate child. I have brought in a governess and a tutor for her, but…'

'She is difficult?'

He nodded. 'But…getting better, I hope.' Each word was breathy with the pain he felt and he hated his exhaustion.

'She looks just like you.'

He smiled. 'I know.'

'She did not wish to leave your side when you were shot. Perhaps if she was allowed in to see you she might be more inclined to behave?'

'Was she hurt?'

'No.'

'Were you?'

She shook her head, but that was not right for he held a vague memory of someone kicking her whilst she lay across him. When she leaned forward she did so with a good deal of stiffness.

'Papa has sent over two men, one as a guard at the front of the house and the other one behind it just in case anyone should have the temerity to try to snatch her again. The place is like a fortress.'

Swallowing, Francis pulled the sheet up about his chin, a small protection of defence against the telltale marks at his throat. No doubt Sephora had seen them already, but still… His hand looked bruised, pointing to the days he had been in this netherworld of pain and semi-consciousness.

He had to regather strength and the will to decipher all that had happened. His wedding had been ruined. That thought bit into everything with a sharp truth.

'I am sorry, Sephora.'

She frowned. 'For what?'

'Your wedding day was…spoilt.'

'I hope I am not so shallow as to think that is more important than your recovery.'

He smiled, liking her honesty. 'Thank you for keeping Anna safe.'

The anger at such an attack on his family consumed him and he was glad for her solid presence. He needed to be better and to be up dealing with things. He needed to find out who had hurt them all and what this meant. When he breathed in, he could smell violets on his wife's skin and was comforted by the scent. But the blackness reached out again to claim him even as he tried to fight it.

He was asleep again and so suddenly. Sephora could see it in the even rise and fall of his chest. Such a repose needed to heal all the ravages the bullet had wrought upon him. Francis St Cartmail was not the father of Anna but her guardian and she was his cousin. The relief when he had told her that was still gathered inside her, bubbling upwards and making her smile.

His eyelashes were long and thick and sat against his cheeks in a dark soft swathe, though the old scar held only brutality and pain.

Contrasts.

He was an earl of the *ton* who knew how to use a knife in a way few men of his station did and the whispered secrets of his past were at direct odds with the respectability and solid history imbued in his family title.

Yet in the disparity Sephora could feel something inside herself shift and grow, a strength and fortitude returning as a life balanced in jeopardy forced her to appreciate all that was still left.

His ring on her finger caught the light and she turned it so that the face of it came within her palm. When she closed her hand she felt the gold warm inside.

She'd been living in a vacuum for so long now with Richard that she had forgotten what it felt like to be so vitally aware of both the good and the bad. To feel so deeply had its barbs, but it also held excitement and purpose and possibilities. Her whole world had changed from the utter boredom and ennui of a week ago to one where the terrifying pace of her adventures left her gasping.

But alive in a way she had never felt before.

'Please, God, let Francis be better soon,' she prayed, sitting quietly as the day darkened into dusk and a chorus of birdsong was heard.

Chapter Eleven

The story of the attack on the earl on the busy London streets was all over the broadsheets and the papers. Other stories had also surfaced about his past, the affair at Hutton's Landing and a fight he had been involved in in Boston. It seemed as if every man who had once held a gripe against Francis St Cartmail was out in force making his voice heard, and Sephora could do nothing to stop the tide of growing complaints

Her parents came to see her the next morning, their faces twin countenances of worry and alarm.

'There is still time to get out of this marriage, Sephora,' her father said. 'Non-consummation of the vows are enough of a reason for the dissolution of the contracts. Any judge would see to it.'

'It is just so very awful,' her mother continued where her father left off. 'You have always been surrounded by beauty and fine living and now…now there is just base rumour and a danger from people who might attack you in the street in broad daylight. We worry for you. We want you to come home and to be with us, to be safe, and back where you belong.'

Her parents' heartfelt litanies after nights of sleeplessness were daunting.

'Richard's mother came up to London the other day, too,' Elizabeth continued. 'Josephine says that her son thinks he has made a terrible error in his judgement and wonders if you might meet him again, to talk sensibly over all that has happened. Perhaps you could resolve your silly arguments and—'

'No.' That word was torn from absolute certainty. 'I have no wish at all to go back to what I was.'

'Then this is enough? This slander against your name. This uncertainty? It is said that it was Douglas's illegitimate daughter who was being dragged away on the street. A daughter from an affair he had with some woman of the night.'

'Well I can tell you now that is false. Anna St Cartmail is the earl's cousin. He is her guardian and has brought in a well-thought-of relative to look after her. It was not his fault that she was in danger on the streets of London and I am certain that he will see to things once he is better…'

'But will he be? I heard he had been shot at point-blank range. How does one survive that, Sephora, and live a full life afterwards?'

'With resolve, Mama.'

Her mother extracted a handkerchief from her reticule and blew into it. 'Maria said we should not be able to change your mind, but if you ever find yourself wondering what to do…'

'I shan't.'

'Do you need money, my dear, to help you through this time?' Her father's words were quiet and firm.

'No, Papa. We have more than enough.'

At that moment a filthy, huge, wet, grey dog tore around the corner of the salon, its matted mangy fur standing up against a bony spine and yellow teeth exposed. Before they could all leap out of their seats, though, the housekeeper was in the room, her clothes soaking and soap on her face.

'Miss Anna and I are giving him a bath, my lady. Lord Douglas said to bring him in and feed him, but he was just so very unclean...' She stopped as she saw Sephora's parents and swallowed, but the dog leapt past her again, its paws skidding on the shining parquet floor into the direction of the kitchen, Sephora thought, and the answering shout from Anna St Cartmail told her that the guess had been correct.

'Well, I think we have probably seen enough.' Her mother was on her feet and her father beside her. 'I can't imagine what might happen next and I hope, Sephora, if you are honest with yourself, you may not be able to either.' She sounded breathless and her words were tight, but at least she was no longer crying. Her father joined her and then they were gone, the silence of the room broken only by the howls of a dog who had obviously been dumped into a tub of water and was being cleaned spotless to within an inch of its life.

Francis was awake when Sephora looked into his room a few moments later. He was sitting on the side of his bed and had a shirt on, the thick wedge of bandage showing through the linen.

Several drawings of dogs were stacked on the bedside table. They were well executed, although the animal in pencil looked a lot more regal in bearing than the one she had just seen in the flesh.

'Anna drew them for me. She came in to see me very early and when the dog howled close by I asked her to see it was given something to eat. It is the first conversation that has been pleasant between us since she came.'

'She would be thankful you saved her, no doubt, and mindful of the fact that you nearly gave your life to do so. You seem better today?'

He gestured to a bottle of medicine. 'The doctor left me something stronger for the pain and combined with the brandy Daniel brought in, it must be working.' His humour was comforting.

'And these?' More drawings were in a pile on the coverlet, giving the impression that he had been shuffling through them.

'My ward is doing her best to convince me the animal appears more attractive than I imagine he is. I said that she could feed it a bone from the kitchen, but I gather from the noise I just heard it has made its way into the house already and Mrs Wilson has seen it.'

'It is being given a bath as we speak.'

'What sort of dog is it?'

'A large grey mangy one with yellow teeth and an old ill-healed wound right along its back.'

He smiled. 'I don't think you are convincing me to keep it.'

'Mama and Papa arrived just as it came indoors, a wet and soaking pile of smelly fur. They left as soon as they could.'

'Because of the dog or because of me?'

She could not lie. 'Stories are swirling around London about your involvement in things that are…'

'Dubious. Questionable. Suspect.'

'Yes.'

'And your parents are worrying how the "angel of the *ton*" has managed to get herself caught up in the less-than-salubrious affairs of a disreputable earl?'

Sephora smiled. 'I doubt people call me that any more and I am glad for it.'

'Glad?'

'The pressure of being always good is probably as stultifying as the one you bear of being always wicked.'

He laughed and a hand went to his injured side, his breathing rough and quick.

'There are always two sides to every story, Sephora.'

'Then who was Ralph Kennings?' She watched with a growing disquiet as a flush of anger crossed over his humour, cancelling it out.

'Who told you about him?'

'Maria. She said you were with Adam Stevenage's cousin out at Hutton's Landing and that Kennings tried to murder you.'

Hell, he had not expected Sephora to know that name and the shock of it made his heart beat so fast Francis could feel the blood throb around the bullet hole in his shoulder.

'Ralph Kennings is a man I killed. I shot him three times, once through each knee and then a third time through the heart. He had not drawn a weapon.' Better to say it with nothing missing. Better to let her understand just how much he had lost of himself out there in the canyons above Hutton's Landing.

'Why?'

The face of Seth Greenwood came to mind, gasping his last in the mud below the ruined platform, a bullet deep inside him and his blood turning the water scarlet. But it was not that death that Francis dwelt on.

'He'd killed two children and their mother before he came upon us. He wanted gold.'

'Who were these people? These children?'

'Seth's family. He had twin boys. They were babies, for God's sake, barely walking.'

He could not tell her it all. He did not tell her what had been done to him that evening after the platform had collapsed, but the rope burn at his throat tightened about the little there was left of his breath. He could see the horror in her eyes, the brittle shocked blue even as he wondered what was reflected in his own.

This was the truth of him, the brutality and the tragedy. Thinking of Hutton's Landing negated any softness or goodness that he might have nurtured had he walked the finer line of gentility.

'Your parents want you home, no doubt? They want you safe and well away from me? Perhaps they are right.'

But she shook her head and drew in breath,

holding it until she spoke again. 'Life would be different, then, in the Americas? Wilder. Savage, even.' He could hear the hope of it in her voice.

'Honour is honour, Sephora, and mine was lost there in those three easy shots. I was a marksman in the army and damn good at my job. I knew I would not miss.'

'Why are you telling me this? Why do you not defend yourself when you can only suffer from the consequences?' She stood and her hands were shaking, wound around each other in front of her, every nail bitten back to the quick.

'Because I should have told you of it before we were married. Because I am not the safe harbour you imagine me to be and your sins in the eyes of the *ton* are nowhere near as dark as the guilt I hold. I ought to have given you a choice, to have me or to not, and I didn't and for that I am sorry.'

She looked as if he had struck her.

'Richard never apologised to me once in all the years of knowing him and I didn't expect him to either because by then I'd lost whatever it was that gave me worth.'

'Worth?' He could not quite understand what she meant.

'Opinions. Beliefs. The ability to say no and to mean it. People can die by small degrees just as easily as they can by the quick slam of a bullet and sometimes justice isn't so easily measurable. Those murdered would most certainly think your honour intact given your actions and even the Bible has its verses urging an equitable vengeance.'

'An eye for an eye?'

'And a life for a life.'

Unexpectedly she leaned down and took his hand in her own, tracing the lines across the inside of his palm in a gentle touch. 'You saved mine in the water under the bridge and also perhaps out of it. Is there some sort of celestial scales, do you think, one that places human souls in arrears…or not?'

'The thought is tempting.' He liked her reasoning. He liked her smile. He liked the quiet sense she spoke and her conviction.

'If it were left to me to decide, yours would be a balanced tally sheet. And with Anna…' Dropping his hand, she pointed to the thick bandages under his shirt. 'With this I would imagine you are now ahead.'

He'd never had another person who believed in him like this, someone who would hear out his worst confessions and come up with an answer that made sense.

'Strong opinions are always valuable, Sephora, and if Richard Allerly only wanted to hear his thoughts parroted back by those around him then he is more of a fool than I took him for.'

She smiled, but he could see she was not happy. 'I believed I deserved what he gave me in the end. I think sometimes I didn't even want a different life because I wouldn't have known what to do with it.' She told this unexpected truth flatly, as though what she described had happened to someone else; a public truth rather than a private one.

'And now?'

The fierce anger was unmistakable. 'Now I am different.'

'Good for you.'

When she laughed the sound of it ran through the memory of three shots high up above the canyons near Hutton's Landing. Sometimes at night Francis imagined he had seen Kennings go for his gun, there on his hip just before he had fired, the movement against a silver dawn small but real. Today he hoped that this was true for her sake as well as for his own.

'The doctor said I would be well enough to travel down to the family seat in Kent in a few days.'

'I'd like that.'

He felt some of the tension inside him ease. His wife would come with him even knowing about Kennings? Being in the country would give him some time to work out how to protect Anna, too, and away from the gossip of the *ton* he wouldn't have to worry about what other things might reach Sephora's ears.

The tiredness that had consumed him since the accident needed to go. He wanted his energy back to look after the family he had somehow been gifted with.

The screams in the night woke her, shrill, loud, screams with desperation imbued in every one.

Coming to her feet, Sephora ran into the room down the corridor to find Anna sitting up in bed white as a sheet and covered in sweat.

'I am fine.' The curt voice was underlined by blind fear.

'Well, you do not look it to me and when I am worried about something it is always so much easier when you have a friend beside you to share it with.'

Taking her hand, Sephora sat down beside the girl, holding on even as she tried to pull away. Anna's fingers were as freezing as they had been the last time Sephora had held them. It was as if the blood had not reached them at all in its course around her body, but left her shivering in the extremities. A child made frozen by anger.

'You are safe, Anna. There is nothing here that will hurt you. I promise.' She knew the instant the dreadful terror receded for the long and thin fingers relaxed. The girl's fear was heartbreaking, a child with demons snapping at her heels and enough fury to keep others at bay.

'If they come here to get me, you won't let them do it?'

'I won't.' Sephora was not quite sure just who Anna meant, but now was not the right time to dwell upon it, the child's heart beating so fast she could see the lawn of her nightgown going up and down. 'You belong to us now, to this family. We will never let you go.'

'No one has wanted me to stay anywhere with them before. Clive said he did, but he never meant it. Not at the end.'

Sephora had no idea who this Clive was or where the child's mother had gone, but she squeezed the thin hand and stayed quiet.

'This is the first house where I have my own room. And books,' she added. Small fingers still held on tightly. A lifeline perhaps, a raft across the deeper waters of her past?

'You helped me in the street. The man kicked you, I felt it, but you still didn't let me go.'

Tears now trickled down her face, the beauty of the Douglases stamped on her, too, but so much harder to see in the anger and under the ill-shorn lanky hair.

'If Uncle Francis had died...'

'Well, he didn't. He is making good progress and by tomorrow I think he will be up and about once again.'

'You are certain of it?' For the first time the girl made true eye contact, the dark green of the earl's own eyes looking out at her.

'Most certain. But we need to get you to sleep

now so that you have some energy for that stray
dog I saw you with today. He will be scared by
all the change and worried you will send him
away so you'll need to be calm and kind when
you handle him.'

'Like you are? With me?'

Sephora blushed in pleasure. 'People come
to others in different ways, Anna. Dogs, too.
Sometimes in life there is no reason for things,
but it just feels right.'

The girl smiled and as she tucked down under
the blankets again Sephora began to hum some
of the songs her mother had sung to her when
she was young. A movement by the doorway
had her turning and Francis St Cartmail stood
there, leaning against the frame for balance,
fresh blood staining the linen of his shirt where
it had seeped through the bandage. He gestured
to Anna, asking silently of the young girl's welfare, and when Sephora nodded he was gone.

She wondered at the pain and determination
such a foray must have cost him even as she
kept on singing, his Douglas stubbornness an
exact copy of Anna's.

A few moments later she looked into the
earl's room. He was sitting on a chair with a

cloak around himself and the chamber was freezing. Every window was open.

'She's asleep?'

'Yes. I promised her that she belonged to us now and that we should never let her go. Is that something I should not have?'

'Did such a troth feel like the right one to give?'

Tipping her chin down, she looked him directly in the eyes. 'It did.'

'Then there is your answer.'

'You truly think it that simple?'

'I do.'

As she was about to speak again a movement beneath his bed by her feet made her start. 'The stray dog is in here?'

He nodded and smiled. 'Take him into Anna's room and place him on her bed. If she wakes again, he will afford her comfort.'

'Does the dog have a name?' she asked as she bent to take hold of the new leather collar around the animal's scrawny neck.

'Hopeful,' he replied. 'I've called him that.'

Lying alone in bed a few moments later, Sephora watched the moonlight on her ceiling. She was happier here in a household filled with problems than she had been for years. There was a scrawny, abused dog lying entwined in the warm arms of an orphan child who suffered nightmares down the corridor one way and a man who held his own demons close and his past even closer down the other. Each had their secrets and their terrors. Each held the world at bay in silence and in anger. But beneath all that was difficult she felt the beginning of everything that could be easy.

Francis had called the dog Hopeful. She smiled at the name as she fell asleep and dreamed of water.

Maria and Aunt Susan came the next day and the one after that, too, and it was late on the second afternoon that her sister mentioned she had seen Richard Allerly at a small private function she'd attended with Mr Adam Stevenage.

'He had his arm entwined in that of the oldest Bingham girl and he was back to hovering. Miss Julia Bingham looked as though she was a cat who had just found the cream, though I suppose she may not be as pleased with herself in a year or two when she manages to determine the Duke of Winbury's true character and rues the loss of her own.'

'Poor girl,' Sephora returned, glad that Aunt Susan was out of earshot over on the sofa. 'If I thought it could make a difference I might even feel the need to warn her off him. As it is I am going to just wish them the best.'

Maria turned to look at her. 'You have changed and I like it. Mama said you would not last a month in such a madhouse, but I think you will never leave the Earl of Douglas because you are happy. He makes you such even trussed up in bandages and lying in a sick room.' She began to laugh. 'I happily admit there is a strength in the man that is beguiling, and a sensuality, too. Imagine his effect on your person when he is well.'

Sephora shook such nonsense away, though part of her had been imagining the very same thing. 'Papa looked tired when I saw him?'

'He is still not speaking to Winbury at all and only a little to Aunt Josephine, which is surprising, and that is taking a toll. I think he wants to wait and see what happens here before he makes his mind up.'

'Tell them I am happy, Maria. Tell them if I

had the chance to change anything at all that I would not.'

'Adam says Francis St Cartmail is a genius in his business dealings and hopes he might take him on as a partner in his manufacturing businesses up north. He also said that Douglas sent his cousin's mother money after Seth Greenwood's death, enough money to be comfortable for the rest of her life.'

Sephora was pleased to hear this. 'Richard always told everybody what he was going to do and never did it, whereas the Earl of Douglas seldom says a word and quietly sees to everything.'

'I think you love him.' It wasn't a question.

Turning away, Sephora felt a sort of hopeless longing. 'I was ruined. Surely that is enough of a reason to at least be grateful.'

'You lied to yourself every day when you were with Richard. I hope you are not still doing it.'

'Maria?'

'Yes?'

'I will miss you.'

Francis was up the next morning, dressed and eating a hearty breakfast when she came downstairs. 'Daniel Wylde is in town with his wife, Amethyst, and they have asked us to a celebration at their place in the afternoon.'

'A celebration?' She didn't feel up to the whole social gambit yet and was certain that he wasn't. They had not discussed any arrangements particular to their marriage either and when they spoke now she felt more and more as if they were strangers.

'Lucien's sister, Christine, will be there and the Wesleys, Gabriel and Adelaide Hughes. A small occasion to mark our wedding though unfortunately Lucien and his wife, Alejandra, are away in Bath on holiday.'

These people were all Francis's best friends and she was nervous of any questions that might come her way, for so far Francis and she had been circling around each other, a few truths that were surprising, and then long times of polite distance. She wondered what he might have said of her privately.

Women, too, had their ways of finding out things and although she had spoken with Adelaide Hughes and Amethyst Wylde briefly at different social events, she did not know Christine Howard at all, though she had seen her at a distance. She had never had women friends as such, Richard taking up most of her spare time.

So many thoughts made her dizzy and she helped herself to a cup of tea and sipped it slowly. 'I hope they will like me.'

Francis looked up at that and frowned. 'Why would they not?'

'Perhaps they might think…' She stopped for a second, but made herself carry on as he raised his eyebrows. 'They are strong women. I imagine that there are things about me that they cannot admire.'

'Such as?'

'Arriving at your house alone and uninvited and getting drunk on whisky. Tricking you into offering marriage to save me from a ruin of my own making.'

His laugh was rough. 'You truly think that of me? That I could be tricked into something that I did not wish to do? Something as important as marriage?'

'I don't know. I am certain you wouldn't have been interested in pursuing an acquaintance with me if I had not forced the issue, but…'

Now all humour had fled and he looked deadly serious. 'This damn bullet has so far ripped out any chance of showing you exactly what marriage should mean, Sephora, but I am recovering. Do not expect such a state of grace to last much longer.'

With that he stood, upending his cup of strong coffee before setting it down, dark eyes running across her in a way that was disturbing. He was newly shaved and his hair had just been washed and any of the illness suffered over the last week seemed to have run away with the bathwater.

A virile man with his own needs and beautiful beyond measure. Even the thought of it made her cheeks blush.

'If it's any consolation my friends were all trying their hardest to get me to see you as a suitable candidate for a bride long before you agreed to marry me.'

Then he was gone.

The afternoon began badly as the rain that had been holding off for the morning suddenly bucketed down on the small run between the carriage and the front door of the Wyldes' town house. Her hair was ruined, despite the umbrellas, of that she was sure, the curls so carefully fashioned hanging down the front of her jacket in long damp strands.

Francis St Cartmail on the other hand looked magnificent, the rain on his face and scar curled into laughter. 'God, I love England,' he said with feeling as they were shown inside. 'In America, for a good part of it, there was nothing but heat.

'Rain suits you, too,' he added as he took her cloak and passed it on to a waiting footman. 'I like your hair less…formal.'

And after that it was easy, Daniel Wylde's wife taking her hand and leading her into the room, a warm welcome on her face.

'We have been looking forward to meeting you properly, Sephora. Might I call you that? Francis has been alone for a large number of years, you see, and I always hoped that marriage would be his saving grace.'

As Lady Adelaide Wesley came forward Sephora remembered the last time they had spoken was on the subject of her marriage to the Duke of Winbury, the 'body, soul and heart' talk that had left her flustered and afraid.

Today, however, she was smiling and after searching for a moment in her reticule she lifted up a small bottle of oil.

'For fertility,' she explained. 'I give some-thing to every new bride I know and chart which of the potions works the quickest. I have much hope in this elixir so I pray you don't disap-point me.'

The general laughter accompanying this statement meant Sephora's embarrassment went largely unnoticed.

Lucien's sister, Lady Christine Howard, was the next one to be introduced. Sephora had often seen her at a distance in society and admired her grace and beauty.

'I am so pleased to meet you, Sephora, and I do love your dress.'

Amethyst laughed. 'Christine has a business designing and making wonderful gowns though it is rather a secret.'

'Business?' Sephora had never really known a woman in business in her life. The idea of it was truly revolutionary.

'We are not quite the normal run of the women of the *ton*, Sephora. We like to fashion our own paths and woe betide the man that tries to stop us.' It was Amethyst Wylde who gave this explanation, quietly but honestly.

Goodness, Sephora thought as she digested

this last confidence. She was so much more used to flighty small talk at social occasions, unimportant musings or even the more pointed gossip, and she could not believe the way this conversation was heading.

These women were…powerful, that was the word she sought, powerful in their hopes for themselves and each other, fearless in their opinions and she liked it. Maria would like them, too, she thought, and wished her sister could have been there.

At that point Gabriel Hughes lifted his glass to make a toast.

'Here's to a long and happy marriage,' he said. 'The final penniless lord and the last one to find his bride.'

'To Francis and Sephora.' Daniel Wylde spoke now and in the gaiety Sephora looked over at Francis and saw him watching her.

'To us,' he said quietly and handed her a glass. *'Ad multos annos.'*

The Latin made her smile though she wished that he might have made some mention of love.

Francis came to her room late that night, knocking on the closed door and waiting until she opened it. She was in her nightgown with a thick woollen shawl across her shoulders and some bright red slippers Maria had knitted her for her last birthday on her feet.

'I found this on the shelves of my library and I thought that you might like it,' he said and when she looked down she saw he was holding a book, bound in leather and embossed. 'It was given to me a long time ago and I remember you told me when I was sick that you wrote stories.'

When he handed it to her she saw it was a journal, each page embellished with small figures from fairy tales and beautifully executed.

She wanted to ask who had given him this, but something in his eyes stopped her. He looked lonely, his hair tonight loose so that it sat around his shoulders in long dark curls. His stock was loosened, too, and across the top of the linen she saw a small portion of the scar that traced from one side of his throat to the other.

'I am just having a hot drink. Perhaps you might join me?'

He seemed perplexed and for a fleeting second Sephora thought he might refuse, but then his reserve softened and he nodded his head. In the midst of her chamber he was hard, large and masculine and she was glad for the chairs before the fireplace to direct him to.

Pouring tea, she watched him take up the dainty china cup and smiled, for she could smell a stronger libation on his breath. Brandy, perhaps, or whisky.

'This room used to be my sister's,' he said after a moment and the shock of the information had her placing her own cup down.

'I thought there was just you in your family?'

He shook his head. 'No. I had a sister, too, who was six years older than me. Her name was Sarah. She was in London at her school on the day our parents died.'

'And you. Where were you?'

'I had been sick for a number of months with a chest infection and was recuperating at Colmeade House. After that I was never ill again. Not with that particular malady anyway.'

'Who came to tell you about what had happened?'

His eyes skirted away from her, but not before she had seen the pain in them.

'No one. They did not return that night or the next one. Finally a friend of my father's arrived to let us know.'

'Us?'

'The servants and me. The family lawyer came down the next day and I was quickly returned to school.'

'Just like that?' She was horrified and furious and she could hear the anger in her voice. 'To just send off a small grieving child like a parcel and expect him to be all right? It is archaic and dreadful and if I ever have a baby I should hope that—' She stopped when she realised what she was saying and thumbed through the pages of the journal with shaking fingers.

'It was my sister's, but she died shortly after my parents did. It's embossed with her initials, but as they are now the same as your own I thought you might like it.'

S. St C. Sarah. Sarah St Cartmail. Francis and Sarah St Cartmail.

All the little pieces of the Earl of Douglas were beginning to get filled in. Like a puzzle, this bit explaining that one and the tragedy of his past overshadowing everything.

What was it Amethyst Wylde had said today? *'Francis has been alone and I always hoped that marriage would be his saving grace.'*

He'd lost so many people and was still losing them. No wonder he had tried so hard to make sure Anna was safe when she was snatched in the street. Even his kindness to the homeless mangy dog began to have an explanation for he'd probably felt like that, too, as a child. Nowhere to go. No one to love him. She wondered how his sister had died, but did not like to ask.

'If I began to write stories again, could I read some to you?'

He looked up at that and smiled 'You'd want to?'

'Only if you did not laugh at them or tell me to stop writing.'

'Seth Greenwood used to pen tales about gold and the fever of it. He even had one published in the Hutton's Landing newspaper. He got a Draped Bust Dime for his efforts and had it mounted in a piece of old polished swamp wood with the eagle side up. I brought it home for his mother.'

'What was he like? Adam Stevenage's cousin?'

'Larger than life and full of it. I met him in New York when I first arrived in the Americas. He was working in steel, but had always dreamed of the gold and so with the last of my money and a tip he'd had from a dying priest, we headed south. We hired a wagon to make it easier for his wife and children and went down the Fall Line Road between Fredericksburg and Augusta. Three weeks later we were ready to pan on the banks of the Flint in Georgia. The same river he died in.'

Sephora was intrigued by the world described, and she was reminded of her uncle's dream of seeing foreign lands and different oceans.

'Not too many weeks ago a man on his deathbed told me that the biggest lesson in life was to find passion. It seems like at least Seth found his.'

Francis nodded and stood, the scar on his cheek caught in the light of the lamp above his head, but his eyes were soft. 'The money from the gold allowed me to invest in manufacturing and save the Douglas properties, but I'd give it all away to have Seth and his family back.'

Without thought Sephora touched him, laying her hand across his and feeling the warmth.

'I want to leave London for Colmeade House the day after tomorrow. It's time I took you home.'

* * *

The next day Sephora received a note from her mother asking her to come and see her in the afternoon, but when she walked into the blue salon of her parents' town house her heart fell.

Richard Allerly was sitting talking with Elizabeth and when he saw Sephora he got up, a smile upon his face. Her mother had also risen and was speaking quickly.

'I thought that the time had come to put all our cards on the table so to speak, my dear, and facilitate some sort of dialogue in order to clear things up between you two.'

'Clear things up?' Sephora could not quite understand what she meant, but Richard was quick to jump into the fray.

'I realise that I was rather remiss in allowing our relationship to falter and I have been hearing a number of unsettling things about your new husband which, to be honest, I could no longer keep to myself. Your mother is as worried about you as I am.'

When she did not speak he carried on.

'Douglas may have been a war hero in Spain, but he certainly seems to have made a mess of his time in the Americas. Not only was he tried

in a court of law there for killing one man, but
he was also rumoured to have hunted and shot
another. He is a dangerous reprobate and there
is no telling what he might indeed do to you,
should he be inclined to.'

'Who told you of this?' She tried to keep her
voice steady, but was so furious she wondered
how she could even form the question.

'It is common knowledge all across London. People are looking at you with pity in their
eyes—the duped bride who has no idea of the
monster to whom she is now married.'

'I see. Where is Papa?'

'He has gone to see his sister and will not be
back till the day after tomorrow.' Her mother
answered this question, her voice tight.

'And Maria?'

Now Elizabeth looked less certain. 'She is
in Kew Gardens with Mr Stevenage and Aunt
Susan.'

'Then it is a shame that they are not here,
Mama, because I would have liked them all to
hear what I have to tell you next.'

As she took in a shaky breath Richard crossed
the room and threaded his arm through her own.
'Come, my angel. I think you need to sit down

for you look flustered, pale and upset and I re-alise that this is all a shock, but…'

The same feeling she had had for so many years came upon her just at his words. He gen-erated a weakness in her, a worry and a fear that was so familiar she almost felt sick. The woman she had been might well have sat and been fussed over, all her insecurities rising like butterflies off a summer tree. But she had changed and the new her was nowhere near as accommodating to perceived failings.

'Please do not touch me.' She waited until he had taken a step back before she went on.

'I shall not be commenting on the stories about the Earl of Douglas, Richard, but I will say that I know the circumstances surrounding them because my husband himself has told me.

'I will also say that for years now I have been unhappy and frightened, of you and me, of us together. You make me less, Richard, whereas all Francis St Cartmail does is make me more. I can think with him and converse. I can offer opinions and argument and ideas that are far different from his own and expect no redress or criticism. The passion for life which you said I had none of has returned and I thank you for that because without your honesty I may have never realised that my own was so lost. There is nothing you could say, Richard, ever, that would tempt me to be the girl again who I was with you. That girl has gone. She has grown up and become this woman and I like her strength so very much more.'

Her mother had simply sat down on the sofa and Richard looked as if he might strike out, but Sephora smiled through the undercurrents and held herself together.

'I am leaving London for Colmeade House in Kent tomorrow, Mama, and I have no idea when I shall be back, but I hope we will be gone for a while. Maria, no doubt, shall be down to visit and you and Papa are welcome when you can understand that the Earl of Douglas is the man I have willingly chosen to be my husband forever and I have absolutely no regrets about my decision.'

With that she simply turned around and took her leave, a few strides to the front door where she collected her cloak and hat and then down the steps and into the waiting Douglas carriage.

Once there she took in a breath and brought

her shaking hands up in front of her, her marriage ring glinting in the light.

She had done it, she was free, the cloying possessiveness of Richard Allerly behind her once and for all. Every word she had uttered held a truth that was astonishing and illuminating and wonderful. Francis gave her strength and power and the ability to be herself.

Dragging her journal from her bag, she found a pencil and began to write of how it felt to be alive and young and free. To know the passions that her uncle had spoken of on his deathbed, the gifts of life and hope and happiness.

'I'll live life for you, too, Sarah,' she promised, the pad of her finger tracing the embossed initials in the leather of the cover as the whole of her world opened up into new possibility.

Chapter Twelve

Colmeade House came into view finally. She knew Francis had found the journey uncomfortable for she could see a sheen of sweat across his upper lip, although he only smiled at her when she mentioned her concern. Anna on her other side had been turning and squirming for the whole trip just to catch a glance of the carriage behind theirs, the one that was carrying Mrs Billinghurst, her son, Timothy, and the dog.

'Hopeful does not like travelling. He was sick the other day when Timothy took him across London and Mrs Billinghurst said that it is his stomach and that some dogs are born that way.'

'Well, he has another minute or two to last at the most for here is the estate now.' They all looked out of the window at this, the vista of a Palladian-style home greeting them, the stone tinged almost pink in the afternoon sun.

'But it's so beautiful,' Sephora found herself saying, the edge of slight ruin taking nothing from its grandeur.

'My great-grandfather built it, but ever since it's been left to stand against the elements and with the help of passing time and little capital invested in it this is the result. My own father hardly touched it.'

'There is plenty of room for Hopeful to run around in it anyway,' Anna said quietly as the carriage came to a halt. 'Will it be safe for him?'

'It is safe for the dog and safe for you, too, Anna. There is nobody and nothing here to hurt you, I promise it.' Francis said this in a tone that did not brook argument and when Anna smiled at him Sephora could see a softness there that made her look beautiful. Breathing in, she looked away and swallowed back the tears.

The park went as far as the eye could see, falling to a lake in the foreground and a round loggia of sorts far in the distance, the tall trees that bordered the open spaces planted with the idea of creating a pattern of space and gran-

deur. The heritage of the Douglases was as unexpected as it was beautiful. She'd imagined a
smaller estate and one in better condition. This
would need much in the way of time and energy
to see it functioning properly.

She remembered then what the earl had told
her about his not coming home as a child because it was too much of a nuisance to open the
house for one small boy. The boy who would
inherit everything. The child who had been an
orphan just as Anna was one. What must this
place have represented to a son who had just
lost his parents? The missing tiles on the roof,
the aged patina in the stone, the flaking paint
on every window sill observable? Beautiful, but
beaten somehow, rich in its lines of architecture,
but poor in its maintenance.

Timothy had joined them now with the dog
and his mother, Mrs Billinghurst, behind them.
Some of the Douglas servants from town had
come down to Kent two days prior to get everything ready. Sephora was glad Francis had hired
a number of men to make certain the property
was secure.

In front of the wide stairwell those serving

the house had lined up, the aprons the women all wore white and shining in the sun.

'Come, I will introduce you, Sephora. Many of these people have served my family for generations. Mrs Billinghurst will take the children inside for luncheon.'

She wished she might have simply followed them up the wide steps into the house, but came behind Francis to meet his staff. The earl was charming to each of them though she could see the distance he also maintained. A smile here and a question there and then they, too, were on the way up the steps and into the house proper.

He took her into a salon to his immediate left and shut the door behind him, leaning against it and closing his eyes. It had been weeks since the attack in the streets of London and each day he had got better and better, but the long trip had exhausted him. She could see it in the grey tinge on his skin.

Crossing to a cabinet she opened the door and pulled out two glasses and the first bottle that came to hand. 'Drink this. You look as if you need some fortifying.'

Francis smiled when he tasted the tipple. He was sitting now on a wide sofa near the door.

'Whisky?' he asked. 'Seems appropriate some-how. At least if I get drunk you won't have to take me home and as we are already married Winbury will no longer be a problem.'

Their glances met across the small distance and something inside her moved. The wound had stopped him coming to her room in London as he had tried to recuperate, but here...already she could see an expression on his face akin to intimacy.

'I do wish for this marriage of ours to be a proper one, Sephora.'

'Proper, my lord?' She used the words carefully.

'I would want you to sleep with me, every night. It won't be a sham.' He glanced up at her then without any hint of question and she swallowed because suddenly Richard's words were back in her ears echoing around the chambers creating uncertainty.

'You are cold and unfeeling in this way, Sephora. You always have been.'

Was he right? Already her heart was beating faster in worry and she stared at him mutely, unable to formulate any answer at all to explain it away.

* * *

The colour had gone from her face, Francis thought, simply drained like water in a sink at his words. She looked horrified and frightened, not the normal worry of a wife who went to her marital bed for the first time but something else.

'Did Richard Allerly ever…?' He stopped there because she was shaking her head madly. Placing his drink on a table he stood as she answered his question.

'No. He was not like that and I was glad for it.'

'Not like what?' Lord, this conversation was getting away from him and why would she be glad?

'Did he kiss you?'

'Yes.'

'And you liked it?'

'No.' Now her eyes were like wide saucers of pure shock.

'But you loved him?'

'At first I did. A long time ago. After that I was trapped. Everyone just expected us to be together. Like you expect seasons to change or Christmas to come or the organ to be playing in a church on Sundays. No thought in it really just…'

'Presumptions?'

'Exactly. And at the end I hated him.'

This was said so softly he could barely hear her.

'He said…Richard said…I was cold and passionless and had always been that way and I think it is the truth.' Her fingers were clamped into shaking fists, every knuckle stretched into white. 'Once I overheard Papa saying the same thing to my mother. Perhaps it is the sort of weakness that runs through a family and blights it, a fatal flaw like Hamlet with his prevarications or Achilles with his ego. And if so then I am not…'

He reached out for her, simply taking her lips, hard and honest and without hesitation; and if he felt her tremble he ignored it, opening her mouth under his and coming within. To plunder, to taste, to know what it was that lay between them in the shock of their contact, to feel the red hot want of lust and roiling waves of desire that raced inside. To show his unusual new wife that she was not frigid or damaged at all.

And then he broke away.

'Passionless? I do not think you are that.'

But she stood there dazed, with her mouth

open and her breasts heaving and when he registered the voices of Anna and Timothy coming down to them along the hallway he leaned forward and whispered.

'Tonight, Sephora, tonight I promise to show you just what burning feels like.'

It was happening all over again just as it did at the river; one action that changed her perception of the world, one kiss that had made everything different.

And his promise of tonight? The loosening of something inside her made her light-headed and light-hearted and transformed her from the woman she was before to the one she was now. She had felt everything the stories talked of when he had kissed her, the breathlessness, the possibilities, the wonder. The wooden Sephora Connaught had simply melted into a living flame, wanting him, wanting more, and understanding so terribly all that she had missed with a man who had only ever made her feel less.

The dog brushed up against her, his wet nose leaving a trail of darkness on the silk of her skirt. Francis was laughing at something Anna had said and Timothy was chatting to him as

if the Earl of Douglas were the masculine em-
bodiment of everything wonderful.

This was a whole full life given to her when
she had least expected it and risen from the ruin
of her mistakes. She decided that she would
drink whisky with her husband for the rest of
her years and smiled. She was glad that he had
given her the time to recover by distracting the
others though when his gaze came across hers
she remembered again his heated promise.

Tonight. Her eyes went to the clock above the
mantel, only a matter of hours until it came, and
he winked as he saw her interest there.

'Can we walk to the top floor of the house
and see the view?' Anna asked this of Francis.

'Are you scared of heights?'

'No.' Anna's voice was becoming more and
more certain and today her ill-cut hair was held
back by a hairband. It suited her. So did the
smile that came as Francis held out his hand
and she reached for it.

The two of them ate that night at a table set
for a king. There were lilies on the sideboard,
from London Sephora supposed, their scent
heavy and compelling. The silver was well

polished and the plates were Sèvres, bordered in gold and aqua and monogrammed in the middle—the letter 'D' hung with greenery and colourful tiny flight-filled birds.

The Earl of Douglas was almost as decorated as his plates, his jacket of green velvet and his waistcoat of a burgundy-and-saffron-embroidered silk. She had never seen Francis St Cartmail in anything other than dark and sombre hues before and though he looked well in those the bright and striking colours of tonight's garb were breathtaking. The cabochon ruby on his little finger shone against the candles. As if he recognised what she was thinking he lifted his glass in a toast.

"'A wife of noble character who can find? She is worth more than rubies.'"

'I would say a man wrote that line, my lord.'

He laughed and paraphrased quickly. 'My wife of noble character is worth more than rubies and I have found her.'

They both sipped at the red wine after that, a short distraction while they garnered their wits, Sephora thought, and was glad the footman hovering at her shoulder had gone. Hovering as Richard always had. She pushed the thought away and reached for a new question.

'How old are you, my lord?'

'Thirty-four.'

'And you had not thought to marry before?'

'No.' Simply said. The dimple on his undamaged cheek was shadowed in the candlelight and there was humour in his eyes.

'I saw you once before I met you properly. You were in a garden kissing a woman and not all that politely for she looked more than amorous. It was a ball, if I remember correctly, and I had stepped outside for a brief moment to gather air.'

'It is the plight of a bachelor, Lady Douglas, being pounced on like that. But you have rescued me from such folly forever and I thank you for it. I never saw you at all in society. Perhaps it was because I tried to attend as few events as I could justifiably manage.'

This was how flirting worked, Sephora suddenly thought. This cut and thrust of pleasure and coquetry. If she had had a fan she might have flicked it across her face in the practised way she had noticed others manage. A small diversion. A studied amusement.

She felt more beautiful than she ever had before.

'I'm certain I shall have to do so again, Lord Douglas. Rescue you, I mean, for I have heard your name whispered by many hopeful females after all.'

He finished his glass of wine and set it down. 'When I make a promise, I always keep it.'

'That is indeed a comfort, my lord.' She could not quite interpret what he meant by that. The promise of tonight? The promise of forever? The troths were all getting mixed around in her head and in the pit of her stomach another more languid feeling was growing.

She pushed back the lacy golden shawl from her shoulders and saw his eyes flare. This dress had been carefully chosen to be within the barest whisper of modesty. At the time she had sworn she should never have the courage to wear it, but now…

Now she rounded her shoulders and leaned forward, the ample flesh of her breasts pressing against the thinness of fabric. Francis St Cartmail's reaction almost made her smile, but she shook away mirth and concentrated on something far more dangerous.

'Richard Allerly told me he loved me constantly. The words are easy to say, you see, and when I failed to eventually believe in his sentiments I thought I should never ever wish to hear them again. Not like that. Not worthless and without value. Not parroted without any meaning whatsoever.'

'You wish to know in other ways?' His voice was silky and rough, and if they had been sitting closer she might have reached out then and touched him, to hold his fingers tightly in her own.

But distance had its own appeal, too. A suspended moment. A deferred intimacy.

She took another sip of her wine and watched him.

God, his timid innocent wife was turning into a practised siren, in her golden almost nothing sheath of a gown and with her surprising confessions. She knew how she was affecting him and that was the worst of it. He had been chased down by women ever since he could remember, but none who set his blood to boil like this one could, the words of her disclosure on love spilling into disbelief.

She did not wish for him to give her the troth? She wanted to feel it instead, the breathless pull, the intimacy, the scent of desire.

Go slowly, he commanded himself as the betrayal of his body filled unhearing flesh and the shock of connection drew his skin into goosebumps. There was still the whole dinner to get through, the second course only just coming from the kitchens in the capable arms of a handful of footmen bearing platters.

Sephora pulled her lacy shawl upwards at the intrusion and smiled, the fabric settling across fine breasts and hiding the swell beneath gossamer silk. But he had seen. He knew what had been there, was there still. The sweat on his upper lip prickled with heat and he used the starched linen napkin to wipe it away.

He had lost his appetite for everything save her, but she was thanking his man for the portion of meats just served, and he could do nothing but watch.

'It is a wondrous feast,' she said and looked up, the pale blue of her eyes in the candlelight almost see-through.

'It is,' he answered and knew he did not speak of the food.

'Like artistry?'

'Exactly like it.'

When she picked up her eating utensils the light from the chandelier above caught on a tine of the fork, sending beams of colour into her hair.

An angel. His angel.

The thoughts of ravishment dimmed a little under this realisation and settled into a place that was more manageable. He was pleased his serving staff had withdrawn into the kitchen as he had asked them to do.

'I want heirs.'

He knew he had shocked her, but two could play at this game and he'd had far more years of practice.

'How many, my lord?'

Hell, at that moment Sephora Connaught reminded him so much of a seasoned courtesan that he laughed. A surprising twist. He could barely keep pace with the reactions of his traitorous body and he was struggling with the changeover, whereas she seemed to be relishing them.

'Would four suit you, my lady?'

'Two girls and two boys? A considered

choice? Prescriptive. Accounted for.' The smile was in her eyes now, too. She was teasing him, provoking him, taking his words and turning them around into something else entirely. It was so seldom that anyone else had ever managed to do that, that he was speechless.

Shifting back in his seat he took account of what he had learned tonight about his unusual wife. She was beautiful, of course. However the beauty lay not only in her outside appearance, but inside in kindness, humour and honesty. She was also clever, ruthlessly so, a woman who might turn a conversation completely on its head and smile through his confusion.

The third thing worried him the most. She was so damned sexy he felt like taking her then and there on the rug in the dining room in front of a burning fire, just to see how the flame glowed on the white of her skin and the sheen of her breasts and the pale gold in her hair.

'So, you wish for a fruitful marriage without any mention of love? The act but not the words?'

'The truth rather than the falsity.' She was quick with her reply.

'When I see Winbury next time I think I

am going to knock that damn head off of his shoulders.'

She laughed, but quietly, as if in his troth she found a certain solace.

'I would hope that you do not. He is a man whom I have left behind, a weak man I think, and half a lifetime is too many years to regret. If I could ask you for anything it would be for honesty.'

He smiled. 'Honesty can have its bite, too, Sephora. What would you say if I told you I want to take you to my bed right now and show you the true beauty of what can be between a man and his wife?'

She stood then, taking the linen serviette from her lap and placing her fork and knife carefully on her plate.

'I would say, my lord, that I am finished with dinner.'

The Earl of Douglas made her brave and different. He did not hide behind words but said them to her face in a way that she could not fail to understand the meaning. He wanted her and she wanted him, but the wants were not coated in falsity or childishness or arrogance.

She did not shiver or shake or cower either. Perhaps it was the wine or the fire or her meeting with Richard Allerly yesterday. Most certainly it was the look in Francis St Cartmail's eyes and the way he smiled, without any hint of deceit, a man who knew his wants and needs and let her know it too.

He did not move up beside her to thread his arm through her own but waited for her to come to him. Her choice. His acceptance. The superfine of his jacket sleeve beneath her fingers was soft and they went up the stairs without speaking into his bedchamber.

His was a big room; the double-hung French doors leading to a balcony that looked out over the countryside and the lake. But it was not this vista her eyes went to. The four poster bed was hung with tapestries curled onto mahogany rods and plaited with multicoloured ties. The coverlet was of embossed blue velvet to match the shade of the walls. Eight-hour scented candles burned quietly on each side table next to it.

A Lord's bed, an earl's lair, for the whisper of history was imbued in the oil portraits on the walls and in the intricacy of the old wooden carvings.

But he did not rush her. Rather he crossed to a small cabinet and poured out two glasses of wine before drawing her over to an alcove before a fire.

'Here is to you, my beautiful Lady Douglas. May we grow old together in lust.'

She liked his toast, the truth of what he said in his eyes, just as she liked the taste of the wine and the feel of the fire. Draping her shawl across a nearby chair she turned to face him. Perhaps it was her turn now to talk of the truth. She drained her glass and placed it down.

'I have not ever…' Her glance went to the bed.

'Then we will go slowly.'

'And I worry…'

He stopped those words with a finger full drawn against her lips. 'Shh. There are no rules.'

The same finger began to trace a different path, across her top lip and around one cheek before falling to her chin and neck and then lower. She shivered, but it was not from the cold. All she knew was burning heat and closing her eyes against the intensity of him she simply felt. No rules he had said, neither right nor wrong.

The pad of his finger rose across the swell of

her breast and then the flimsy silk was parted
and he found the heavy weight of flesh and measured it in his palm. Relentlessly, quietly, his
fingers now around her nipple, playing with the
nub so that a thousand other feelings burst inside her and she pressed closer.

'Let me have you, Sephora. Let me love you.'
These words were breathed against her skin,
whispered and desperate, the shock of them
crawling up her spine before bursting open.

'Yes.' She found her reply and gave it, her
want the echo of his own and naked with hope.

His teeth came down over one breast, taking
exactly what he willed. A considered vanquish,
a well-thought-out triumph. It was not anxiety
that consumed her now but bliss and her fingers
came through the length of his hair, the tie gone
as it fell down around his shoulders in a thick
and midnight black.

Her husband. Her lover soon. Every thought
melded into one until there was no logic left as
he lifted her in his arms and placed her down
upon the bed.

She was small and he was large. He was dark
and she was fair and in her pale eyes he could

see both acceptance and fear in equal measure. But she lay there still, looking up at him, her bodice falling about her waist, her breasts exposed to the candlelight and the firelight and the moon.

He wanted to see her when they came together. He did. He had never liked the darkness and she was far too beautiful to hide in it.

Pulling the skirt of the golden gown upwards his hand spilled under silk, past gossamer stockings of white, past the satin ribbons at her thigh. Up into the very warmth of her, a single lace barrier that he disposed of quickly before he came in.

She gasped and began to ride him, head thrown back and her bottom rising, no longer fearful only questing, her breath louder, the veins at her neck stretched. He laid his other fingers splayed upon her stomach and pressed down, feeling himself beneath in the flesh of her, detecting movement. Harder. Quicker. Deeper.

She came like a flame burst, all heat and light and burning, the muscles inside tightening as she took what he gave her without reserve, low groans of pleasure breaking over the final stillness. The wet of her ran through his fingers and there were tears on her cheeks and astonishment in her eyes when she opened them.

'Now you are ready for me.'

'There is more?'

He laughed, but the sound held more lust than mirth. 'Ah, Sephora, love, but we have only just begun.'

She watched as he undressed himself, too languid to help. The jacket and shirt came first and then the neckcloth, the snowy unwound whiteness revealing the dark crimson scars beneath.

'From a rope,' he said as he saw she watched him. No more details. No more emotion. Just the plain fact as to what had happened across the terrible truth of the result.

She wanted to reach up and touch him there, to reassure him, to comfort him, but he had moved now to the fall of his trousers and the tug of his shiny black boots. And then he was naked, his skin golden in the firelight, muscle defined and sinew rising. Other old injuries, too, showed up on his body; a slice of wound beneath the reddened injury from the bullet and two more parallel scars at the top of his arm.

A warrior's body, beautiful, strong and defined.

But when her eyes dropped lower she forgot
to think at all, the full and aroused masculinity wondrous and terrifying. She knew what a
naked man looked like because Maria had found
an old broadsheet folded into a book with a lewd
drawing upon it. The illustration on the page,
however, had not quite explained the truth of
flesh and desire in a man like Francis St Cartmail.

Her fingers of their own accord reached
out and touched him, the rock-hard warmth
of smoothness less worrying within her palm,
fitting there as though it was meant. When he
groaned and stretched she knew she was doing
to him as he had done to her and her fingers
explored further. The light touch of knowledge
drawing a picture for her, understanding his secrets.

And then his hand came across her own and
he drew her up against him, the golden sheath
of her gown falling as liquid to the floorboards,
a small puddle of the last veil between them, the
final revealing. She could see it in his eyes that
he thought her beautiful, but it was his hands

that traced her outline, down the side of her breast and on to the curve of her waist and then lower into the warmth between her legs.

This time he simply sat and lifted her onto the hardness of him, slowly slipping in, one inch and then two, until resistance loosened and he was buried far inside.

She cried out as the pain stung, but he did not release her. Rather he moved slowly and by degrees, allowing her the familiarity and the fullness, the feel of him stretched across her flesh until she thought she might simply break open like a peach falling from the fruit tree in the late summer.

Split with ripeness.

He moved again and another feeling warred with the first. Not as sore now, not as hot, and he always returned to that first final deepness.

'Feel me there, Sephora. Feel me wanting you.'

Whispered words, against the heavy beat of her heart and the shallow pulls of breath, the quiet ease of gentling against the sharp edge of triumph.

His other hand grasped her bottom as he began to move, with force, with strength, no soothing movements now but the full measure of lust.

And instead of pain came ecstasy, thin and quiet at first before crouching to spring fully formed into every part of her body, tearing away restraint as she cried out loudly.

But still he did not allow her rest.

'Come with me, sweetheart, come with me now.'

And the light filled her, like honey and sunshine, shimmering through the heat, taking will and purpose and preference, the urgency from him at odds with all that was languid inside of her as he pressed in one last time and stiffened, breath gone and eyes closed against the light, the beaching waves of release covering each of them, pulling them home.

Neither of them moved, still coupled together, a new union rising from the separate.

'Sephora,' he breathed out when he could finally talk. 'I think that you just took me to Heaven.'

And she laughed at that and felt him leave her, a residue of wetness that had her reaching down though his own hand fell to cover hers.

'No. Take me in. Take me inside when you sleep.'

And so with only a gentle push of a different fullness and a slight shift of her body, she did.

When Sephora awoke, Francis was no longer there and the light from the opened curtains told her it was well past her usual time of waking.

The realisation of why had her turning into the pillow. She had been wanton and shameless, the ache in her lower body underlining her thoughts.

In the night, when the stars were still high in the sky, she had reached out for him and drawn him in yet again, startling him into wakefulness as she had played with sleeping flesh until new purpose had formed.

She had sat above him pushing back the covers so their skin was limned in moonlight, the long lines of flesh and bone made unreal somehow by the dimness. He'd kissed her afterwards, his tongue finding hers and they had shared breath and warmth and safety.

Her fingers drew a line across her lips now. She wanted him again here on the ancient bed, here as the clocks ticked on towards the noontime and the outside world lazed in the season's sun.

'Francis.' She said his name out loud, liking the music in it and the softness; the name of one of the angels in the Bible. She smiled thinking of his darkness and the scar emblazoned as a brand across his cheek. She wondered how he had got the mark and made a note to ask him. He had said something of the war in Spain if she remembered correctly and being lost in the mountains outside Corunna. The same war where his primary job had been that of a marksman, shooting the enemy when backs were turned or when they had thought themselves safe.

A dangerous solitary occupation she imagined, cut off from others, left to the elements. She had read the stories of the Peninsular Campaign and seen the pictures. She wished he was here next her so that she might turn and take him in her arms to keep him safe or to feel him inside her making her want things she had never thought possible.

A little later the door opened and he was there fully dressed, back today in unbroken black.

'I wondered when you would wake. You have been sleeping like the dead.'

His eyes were soft, licked in warmth and his hair was back in its severe tie, dragged back off his face.

Reaching up she took his hand and laid it across one breast. The change in temperature between them was startling and arousing.

'I want you.' Her words. Uncensored. Shocking in the daylight. She did not even blink as he watched her but moved up against his hand and pushed all the covers away.

The tangle of her hair and the ruin of the sheets. A fallen angel, shattered by passion.

When he sat and lifted her onto his lap she had no recall of him unfastening his fall as his manhood came within her, no warning, no caution. The ache of it made her arch back, but he did not break his motion, intent on his lesson, his mouth against the column of her throat and biting down.

And this morning he taught her that loving need not always be soft or gentle. The other side of the same coin of passion had its paybacks though and when she bit into his shoulder he came, the hot rush of completion running over the cold shiver of truth. Only with each other were they whole.

Then he laid her back and pulled the covers across her. 'Sleep now, Sephora, until I come again. No one will disturb you.'

And he did come again once in the afternoon and then in the evening to take her in the way he wanted, slow and quiet. It was a netherworld she lived in waiting for him, only breathing until he was there again, the strength of his hands against the sheltered softness of her body.

He rarely spoke and she did not either. She had not asked for the words and he obeyed her. A taken wife used with care until every part of her body became accustomed to his touch.

And when the stars rose amongst the darkness he had food brought to the chamber and he bathed her in a warm and soapy bath and dressed her in a nightgown of fine lawn. The bed was made up too, crisp and new and as he tucked her within it, he kissed her on the forehead and left.

She woke again in the early hours after midnight, refreshed from so much sleep and he was not there. Taking a heavy blanket from the bed she draped it about herself and left the room with a candle to light her way, reasoning that her husband would be downstairs in the library she had seen yesterday.

He sat on a wide leather chair with his feet up on the windowsill and the room was freezing. When he saw her he smiled but didn't move at all. 'I don't sleep well.'

'And you like the cold?'

Each window was full open, and the cloth from around his neck was discarded on the floor, the vivid scars on his throat easily seen in the moonlight.

'Maria told me the story of what happened.' She gestured with her hands. 'Adam Stevenage relayed it to her. I hope you do not mind?'

'It's only a story,' he said suddenly. 'Just words.'

'Can you give me the truth of them, then? I would like to hear it from you.'

Shrugging his shoulders he leaned back, the brutal marks dark in the soft fold of his skin.

'It was near Christmas and it was cold. I remember looking up in the early dawn and seeing a shooting star and wishing on it. Gold, I asked. I wanted gold to come home and live on and to save the Douglas inheritance as well as to show others here that I was not feckless and reckless and dissolute. I wanted enough to start a family with and to know my neighbours; all the things others so effortlessly seemed to manage but which were lost somehow to me.'

His words were made slower with drink. Whisky, she determined, by the little that was left in his glass.

'My partner Seth Greenwood came down in the morning and I was tired. He'd risen warm from the bed of his wife and I envied him that. I could hear his babies crying even at that distance and see the flame of the fire against the glass. A home.' He looked at her then. 'There is a certain appeal in the word, I always thought. More so perhaps because I never had one.'

Leaning forward, he half filled his glass again and she did not try to stop him. Let him lose himself in the arms of drink she thought as she had lost herself in the embrace of passion.

'Kennings came after the day broke, quietly on a down-wind track. I saw him come and thought he was there to talk. The dogs didn't bark though and I should have taken that as a warning. They didn't bark because he had already been to the house and done his business.

'I think he'd cut through the tethering of the

platform against the bank, maybe when we were away the afternoon before registering our claim. Kennings did not know that then. It was only later he'd have realised that it had all been for nothing.'

His eyes met hers. 'And that is the final irony of what did happen. The nothingness. The futility. The empty void of oblivion that held no payback for anyone.

'He shot at us as the rig collapsed. I felt the bullets rifling through the water, five or six perhaps and loaded quickly, but then I hardly think he'd shoot slow with the stakes so high.

'The first two ripped across my arm and the third went into Seth's shoulder. When the water ran red and there was only silence Kennings probably thought he'd done his job and all that was left was to make certain that the claim was his.

'I couldn't lift Seth up out of the water so I stayed there with him. Hours later he slipped away into the river and I was hauled up into the teeth of a furious lynch mob wanting revenge and retribution. Seth's wife had been found by then, you see, and the babies, and Kennings had spread the word that I had done it. Jealousy was the motive, he said, and greed.

'Seth's body was gone with the river somewhere, Kennings bullet in him and I was so freezing I could barely talk enough to give my side of the tale.

'They hanged me from a cottonwood with its bare winter branches and its ragged bark, but they picked the wrong bough and the branch broke. When the lightning came a second later there were those in the group who felt strongly about signs from God and his omnipotent displeasure and so I was brought instead into town, the rope still around my neck and my throat swelling.' He smiled, but there was no humour there. 'If the damn hanging did not kill me then its effects nearly did. And after,' he stopped and swallowed. 'Afterwards breathing at night was always harder and I could not lie down for a long, long while.'

'Even now?'

He nodded. 'Especially now when there are so many more to keep safe.'

Suddenly she understood why there was a gun next to him and another on the flat of the sofa. 'It's Anna? You know who tried to kid-nap her?'

'Only a list of suspects, but I am narrowing it down.'

Panic made her stand. 'It is dangerous, Francis. These people have already shown what they are capable of.'

'Clive Sherborne was running his own sort of books and because of that Anna is in danger from those who knew about it.'

'How do you know this?' She was simply horrified by what he had said. 'Who are they?'

'I've had people investigating Sherborne's murder since it happened. Anna's guardian, Clive Sherborne, had been providing the finance for a number of years to bring spirits in illegally from France, but he got too cocky with the merchandise. He onsold some of the brandy to London pubs at a rate that was more than what it should have been and pocketed the difference. The man who killed him found this out.'

Her mind whirled into a hundred directions and then they all converged into one. She knew the moment he saw the conclusion she had reached as eyes bruised in anger, fell away from her own.

'Anna was there.'

'I think Sherborne was in it deeper than his lawyer realised and it was easier to involve a child in the transactions than another adult who might betray him.'

'My God. The nightmares…?'

'She thinks she is next.'

This explained why she had wanted all the reassurances of never being sent away from them and why she seldom liked to go outside. But it also threw up other worries.

He reached for her then, opening the cocoon of his blanket, his sleeve pulled back in the moonlight and his jacket gone. Positioning her own wrap over them both she came in tight against him in her thin nightgown and felt his utter warmth and safety.

'It's like that time in London,' she whispered and he tilted his head, still watching the landscape before the house.

'What is?'

'You will save her just as you did me.'

The hoot of an owl from a line of trees to one side of the driveway had the edges of his mouth turning upwards. 'It is said that when you hear a bird calling from the west, good luck will follow.'

'Is that west?' she asked and was pleased when he nodded. 'How many would come here if they had the mind to?'

'Only a few. The Free Trade is a communal business, you understand, and there are many in it who wouldn't be there were the government less greedy. Good men, honest men, men who just want to feed their families. Still, every endeavour has those who are less inclined to follow the law and take it into their own hands. Especially with the lure of gold.' He breathed out and looked at her directly. 'I had a letter today.'

The words made her stiffen. 'Unsigned, of course?'

'The missive threatens further retribution to my family should I continue to hunt for the one who hurt Anna.'

'So we shall not be safe until he is caught?'

'Daniel will be here on the morrow. Luce is in Hastings listening to what is being said and Gabe is making a list of the pubs Sherborne supplied in London. We will find them.'

'That is why you were in that fight at Kew, wasn't it? For Anna's sake?'

'Yes.'

'And everyone called you reckless and dissolute.'

'I was never a person to worry about what anybody else thought.'

'But if you are hurt or…' She could not even finish.

'I won't be. There are only a few hours of darkness left until the morning and no one will come when it's light.'

He kissed her then quickly, the warmth of his lips across hers demanding and rough as one hand cupped the swell of her breast. Like a promise. She felt him draw in breath as he let her go, watching again and vigilant.

Outside through the windows the gardens of Colmeade House looked magical, mystical and quiet.

'It is beautiful,' she whispered, snuggling in, the blanket warm but his body warmer.

'It is a fortress,' he returned, 'and none will harm us here. I swear it, on my life.'

'I believe you.'

She wondered where the frightened woman of a few weeks ago had disappeared to, for if anyone was to come and hurt Francis or Anna she would kill them with her own bare hands. She swore to the heavens that she would.

And so they sat there until the morning, sometimes speaking, oft-times not, and the old stray joined them just before the dawn, like a guard dog, his ears pinned back as he listened in wariness.

She smiled to herself as the sun rose across the hills bathing the land in pink and yellow. She would never have seen the birth of a new day as the wife of a duke. She would never have lain in the arms of half slumber as she was doing now, the blankets warm and Francis's body strong around her own.

She loved him. She had known that for a long while now, but if she had instructed him not to give her the words then she could hardly whisper them herself. But she did inside, as an aria and a melody, her fingers threaded through his and the breath he took mingling with her own.

This was life as it was supposed to have been lived, fearless, brave and uncompromised. The diamonds in her wedding ring winked in the light of the morning and she liked the promise of warmth in the air.

Chapter Thirteen

Sephora watched Anna the next morning as the girl came down the stairs, the dog Hopeful back on her heels and Timothy not far behind.

She was thin and the lines of worry still marked her brow, but she seemed happier nonetheless, more childlike as she giggled watching Timothy attempt a cartwheel and failing. Here at Colmeade House Francis had insisted the son of Mrs Billinghurst be given a position of companion for his ward. The idea had seemed to be working well and the two of them were becoming good friends.

'What had you planned to do today, Anna?' she asked from her place at the table. Francis had not come down to breakfast yet and she imagined he would be trying to catch up on at least a few hours of sleep before their visitors turned up.

'We are building a fort in the attic with all the old furniture left there. Uncle Francis said that we may,' she continued, 'as long as we do our lessons in the afternoon.'

Another day indoors then, Sephora thought. The child never ventured outside either, unless they were with her, and she started each time she heard the noise of a horse arriving at the house. Mrs Billinghurst had also made it known that Anna wet her bed frequently and that she still enjoyed reading in a wardrobe with the doors closed.

Complications and complexities.

Timothy Billinghurst was watching her intently and she smiled, the boy blushing so that the skin on his skull showed red under the fairness of his hair; another child who needed careful handling, lost between the death of his father and the brittle poverty of a genteel mother who had been left with very little on the death of her husband.

'The earl's friends Lord and Lady Montcliffe will be coming today. Perhaps they would be interested in seeing the fort you construct when it is finished. I know I'd like to.'

A little smile from Anna was her reward, but

Sephora had started to treasure these tiny gifts, her heart warming in response.

'There is some silk in my room you might like to use for the windows. If you want to come and get it after breakfast I would be happy to lend it to you.'

'Mrs Wilson already found some velvet,' Timothy replied, 'so we can use that for the walls.'

'A communal endeavour, then.'

Sephora only wished that she might spend the morning tucked up with her husband, in the safe warmth of his arms.

Daniel and Amethyst Wylde arrived after lunch, but the smiling Earl of Montcliffe whom she had met at the wedding looked a lot more serious now and went almost immediately off with Francis to his library, leaving her alone with Amethyst.

'Would you like to walk in the garden with me?' Lady Montcliffe asked, giving Sephora the distinct impression that Amethyst Wylde wanted a place to talk where they could not be overheard or listened upon.

A few moments later out on the pathways

Daniel's wife halted in her observation of the formal gardens and turned to face her.

'I hope you don't mind my asking, but are you aware that the Duke of Winbury has named the date of his wedding to Miss Julia Bingham?'

Surprise was the only emotion Sephora felt at the news. And relief perhaps too, that Richard might have found a woman whom he could love in her stead.

'I didn't know that, but I am happy for him.'

Amethyst stooped to pick a sprig of lavender, twirling it in her fingers so that the scent wafted in the air between them. 'My father used to say that the world is like a pack of cards. Take one away and the rest fall into new patterns. Perhaps this is exactly what is happening here.'

'He sounds wise.'

'Papa passed away a year ago, but at least he saw my children born and he loved them.'

'You did not bring them today?'

'No. We left them with their grandmother because...' She stopped.

'Because they are safer there?'

'Then you know?'

'About Anna and the smuggling ring? Yes.'

'Did you also know that Francis received a

medal in the Peninsular Campaign under Moore for his skills in shooting? He kept a whole regiment from being wiped out by allowing them safe access across a dangerous pass whilst he gave them cover. I should imagine these men will be child's play for him. Besides he has Daniel, Gabriel and Lucien to help him now. He is not alone.'

'Thank you.'

'And you are not alone either, Sephora. If you ever need advice or help you only need ask.'

'I think in the last few weeks I have become a different person to be honest. I used to think I was less than I am now and that it was normal for a man to tell a woman what to do. Richard did that to me and I accepted it, but Francis doesn't and yet…' She stopped.

'Yet?'

'The stakes are so much higher because of it and if I lost him I think I might simply fall to pieces. I am sick to my stomach with the fear of it.'

She had not meant to say as much, but under the gaze of kind dark eyes she found herself pouring out her heart and with little censure.

But Amethyst Wylde only smiled. 'Every

wife who loves her husband feels the same, Sephora. In great love there also resides great loss and who cannot dismiss that.'

'You feel this with your husband?'

'I do, but these men of ours are warriors, and to clip the wings of a hawk is to destroy it. Better to fly alongside them, I always thought, for in knowledge there is less worry.'

'And that is why you came today?'

'It was a part of it although Adelaide also sent me to deliver a stone.' Rummaging in her bag she came out with a sphere of shining crystal. 'She said I was to give it to you for Anna. It is black tourmaline and used to calm fear in a child. She said to tell the girl its protective property will reflect all the bad thoughts of others away from her, like a magical mirror, and that it is the most powerful of the protectors. She also said that the one who owns it must lay the tourmaline in the sunshine every month to ensure its properties stay full and perfect and it is at its most fierce when placed under the user's pillow at night.'

For a moment Sephora could almost hear the unusual Adelaide Wesley saying this, her words blowing on the wind in an echo, and although she had never truly believed in the dark arts she was suddenly touched by the power and the beauty of a gift delivered just when she was most in need of it.

'Can you thank her? Can you tell her I will always be grateful for her thoughtfulness?'

Amethyst smiled. 'I shall make certain to give her your message, but she also sent one for you alone. I was to tell you that the oil she gifted you for fertility was proving a most excellent success and that there had been a record number of twins born in the surrounds of the Wesley estate this year.'

Sephora laughed at this confidence and beneath the walls of Colmeade amongst the scented walkways of an ancient garden she felt a peace that she never had before. This was her home and she was happy.

'I am so glad Francis found you, Sephora. Has he shown you the view here from the parapets yet? No. Well it is more than wonderful although he has never come back here enough.'

'He said as a child he felt a nuisance. Perhaps that is the reason?'

'His sister died at Colmeade House. Did you know that?'

She hadn't because he'd never told her, and

Sephora thought with a heavy heart that everything she had found out about Francis St Cartmail was from someone else relating another awful past tragedy. She wanted to hear the truth from him, what he had felt, how he had managed. She wanted to hold him safe and tell him that she would always be there for him, by his side, and that he was her world and her anchor. All the words she had forbade him to use were sitting on her tongue as she looked towards the house in the hope that she might see him at the window of his library.

The Montcliffes stayed for an early dinner and then they left. Francis looked more relaxed than he had all day and Sephora reasoned he must be making progress with the matter of the smugglers.

Mindful of Amethyst's description of the view from the parapets she asked him to take her up there and a quarter of an hour later they were standing behind a low-slung wall on the very roof of the place, looking over a view that went on forever.

'My father used to come here for hours,' Francis said after a moment or two of watching Sephora at his side take in the majesty. 'He said this vista gave him the space to think and he would bring all his major problems up here to solve them.'

'Did your sister like it here, too?'

'Sarah?' The familiar anger at her loss welled from nowhere and he shook his head. 'No. She didn't like heights. My mother was the same.'

'Amethyst spoke to me of her today. How did she die?'

Her question was quiet but direct and instead of turning the personal away he loosened the stock at his throat and pointed to a thin line of grey a good mile away. 'See that river. It was winter and she had come home for a weekend with my aunt. After the rains the banks around it were swollen and she fell into it…'

He heard her take in a breath, and saw the grief and anguish in her eyes as she spoke.

'Like me? But no one saved her?'

'She was alone. Some people…believe she jumped.'

A small hand threaded through his, holding on tight. 'I don't believe that. If it helps at all I don't think Sarah would have thrown her life away. After all she was your sister, with the blood of the Douglases running through her. Strong blood. Unafraid and brave.'

He smiled at her fervent reply and took in a breath.

'I hope that was the case. I hope the soil just gave way as she was walking. I hope hers was a quick death.' He could imagine her alongside the river, watching the water and thinking. She'd have picked up small bits of flowering plants and old pieces of wood because he could long remember her doing so each time she had taken him with her. 'Perhaps girls need their mothers more, too. Like Anna. Without a guiding hand they might feel…'

'No. You were there and there was still Colmeade House. If she came here it meant that she loved it and perhaps a part of that was that she loved the outdoors. I think it was an accident and there was no one there to save her. Is her death the reason you dived in after me?'

He smiled and looked down at her, her blue eyes tearful and a worry in them that broke his heart.

'I jumped because I knew I had to, Sephora.' He saw her frown, but he knew suddenly that what he said was true. His father had come here to solve his problems all those years before and here he was trying to understand his own.

She believed in him even though many others didn't. She took his fears and put an interpretation on them that was believable and honest, words that made his heart whole piece by piece until his breath came easier. He could talk with her as he had never talked with anyone before.

Bringing her into him he turned her to the view and as the sun went down across the far hills they watched the majesty of it together in silence.

A little while later he spoke again. 'Today I have whittled those involved in the smuggling ring down to only two names. Tomorrow I will leave for London to confront them both.'

'It sounds dangerous?'

He laughed. 'Men of this ilk are always cowards and I have enough skill with a pistol and my hands to easily overcome them if they offer resistance. Besides, I want the chance at vengeance, for what he did to Anna and to us.'

He bent to her neck and kissed the soft sensitive parts with his lips and tongue. She tasted of freshness, soap and violets and when she tried to speak again he simply placed a finger across her lips.

'Make love to me here, Sephora, on the top of the world under the night sky. Just us. Without any other worries. Please.'

'Yes.' Her whisper was firm and he lifted her skirts and came in from behind, the warmth of her enveloping him, taking him in.

The cries were there again, not piercing screams as they had been once before but softer. From his chair by the window in his bedchamber Francis could see Sephora stir, but as he was awake he pulled on some clothes and walked down to Anna's room.

Her chamber was full of light when he came into it, three candles glowing on her bedside table. His cousin was not in bed but sitting on the very end of it.

'I heard you crying.'

Her face was puffy and red as she looked up at him. 'I...am sorry if I woke you up.'

'You didn't. I never sleep well.' He felt at a loss as to what to say next, but Anna helped him.

'Sephora said that you lost your parents when

you were young. Did you ever feel afraid because of it?'

'Not afraid exactly. More angry, I suppose.'

'But you loved them?' She waited till he nodded before going on. 'My mother was hardly ever home, but Clive…was nice sometimes.' Tears ran down her cheeks and she wiped at them with the edge of her nightgown. 'I see things.' This was said very quietly, each word enunciated with an exaggerated slowness.

'What sort of things?'

'I saw Clive when he was killed. He had the money in a bag and he had taken it. A man wanted it back.'

'Where were you when this was happening?' Francis tried to keep the tone of his voice soft, but the fear he could see on her face and hear in her words was worrying.

'Hiding under the hay. Clive told me to stay there and not come out, no matter what.'

'Did you see him? Did you see the man who killed Clive?'

'Just for a moment. He was tall. Clive thought he was a friend, I think, and they talked for a while, but so quietly I couldn't hear what they said.'

'And after?'

'The man left and I stayed hidden for a long time. When it was dark I came out and there was blood...everywhere...and I ran home. The gold was gone and I think he might try to take me away again. I think he wants to kill me, too.'

'I will never let him. I promise you, Anna. You are safe here. To get to you he will have to go through me first and now I know exactly who he is I can find him.'

Her chin began to wobble and she threw herself into his arms, a wet and soft little girl clinging as though her life depended on it.

He'd never been so close to a child before save for Seth's twins, but they were babies and the sobs racking through her made him grit his teeth. Her father had disowned her, her mother had seldom been around and Clive had used her foolishly in order to gain his financial rewards. No adult around her in all her life had been stable and good and true. But he would be. He and Sephora. His arm came around her back and he let her cry until she was finished, the front of his shirt soaked.

Across the room the old dog was yawning and

stretching. 'I think Hopeful is tired and wants to go to sleep. Do you think you can now?'

Anna nodded. 'I like it here. I like my room and I like the books and the wardrobe and the attic at the top of the house. I like my name too. Anna St Cartmail. It means I belong.'

'Good, because this will always be your home.'

'And the man who tried to get me in the city…'

'Will never be able to try again.' As he said this Francis thought there would be a lot more at stake than just the words, but the explanation seemed to give Anna comfort because she scrambled back into bed.

Tucking the sheet up about her chin he bent to kiss her on the forehead. Like his mother used to do to him, he thought, though it had been a long time since he had remembered that.

'Can I blow out the candles now?' He asked her before he left and was pleased when she nodded.

A moment later he was back in his own bedroom. Sephora was sitting on the chair he had been using.

'I heard some of what Anna said. No wonder she is so very frightened.'

'Clive Sherborne knew the man who killed him and Anna said that he was tall. There are two names left on my list and one of them has a disease that has stunted his growth.'

'And the other?'

'A lesser lord of the *ton*, but not for much longer.'

'Would I know him?'

He held his smile and shook his head because he knew that the man was a cousin to the Duke of Winbury and Sephora would know him well.

Terence Cummings. The name hammered under each breath he took. *I will have you tomorrow and you will likely not know what hit you, you bastard.*

Sephora felt a jolt of some worry inside her as Francis turned away, a distant scattered recollection that had her reaching for the sense of it.

'You think this lord is high up in the smuggling chain.'

'I do. He'd have sent those who attacked me at Kew and he was probably there somewhere too, watching and hoping they might have hurt me a lot more than they did. People like that dwell in the shadows and attack in a way that holds no sense of justice and they like to see the results of their handiwork.'

He pulled her up from where she sat and she felt the heat on his skin despite his being out of bed in the middle of the night.

'But come, Sephora, let's warm each other. You are freezing.'

'And will you stay there beside me? All night?'

'I shall.'

He never seemed to feel the cold. Even now with his bare feet and light shirt and trousers he felt as hot as a furnace. She saw he had loosely tied his neckcloth around his throat and smiled. A further protection for Anna. When he shed his clothes to sleep naked she thought again how very beautiful he was.

'What will you do when you find this man?' The blankets were back across them now and she lay in his arms, moonlight falling across the bed.

'I'll teach him a lesson in how not to treat a child and then I will bring him along to Bow Street.'

'Good,' she said and pushed herself up across him to take his lips beneath her own. 'Make sure your lesson is one he remembers.'

Sephora awoke an hour later into full consciousness, her eyes opening and her heart thumping. A lord of the *ton* he had said, and tall. A man who knew his liquor and would travel often. A man who was down on his luck in funds and had dreams of a lifestyle far more grand than his title allowed. A man who felt entitled and hard done by. A man who had been there in the gardens of Kew and would be interested in watching the fight between the Earl of Douglas and the others.

Francis was lying with his head on the pillow beside her, staring up at the ceiling, his feet moving up and down as if in deep contemplation.

'You haven't slept?'

He did not answer.

'What is the name of the lord you suspect, Francis?'

At that he turned, his eyes hard. For a moment she thought he might not tell her anything, as was Richard's way, but then the words came.

'Terence Cummings.'

The truth of the name had her scrambling up into sitting. 'He is a cousin of Winbury's and he was there at Kew. It was him who had led us down that particular pathway in order to come across you, in order to slander your name. He was there in the street in London, as well. I remember that now because I tried to call out to him but he did not come forward. Anna would have recognised him and he knew it.'

Francis took her hand in his own, his forefinger running across the ring he had given her on her wedding day. 'I don't want you involved in this, Sephora. If you were to be hurt…' He stopped and swallowed, but she was not to be silenced.

'Richard did that to me, Francis. He made me less than I could be by his protections and in the end there was nothing left of respect in either of us.'

'What are you saying?'

'I know this man and I know his wife. Cummings's father, Richard's father's cousin, was the second son of a Viscount so he did not inherit much. He needed to work for it.'

'Or kill for it?'

'Can we prove that, do you think? The fact

that he murdered Clive Sherborne for the gold and that he was the one who tried to take Anna?'

'I can goad him into thinking I have the proof until I do, for we are close to finding the paperwork trail he left. But to do so I will have to return to London.'

'Then take me with you to help.'

She hated the way her voice shook with fury and desperation, but she stuck to her intent and stared her husband directly in the eyes.

'Could I stop you?' There was the slightest humour in his tone.

'No.'

'Then let us try to have some sleep and we will leave in the morning. Anna can go to the Wyldes for a time until it is safe for I don't want her anywhere near the man and Montcliffe is impregnable. Celia and Timothy will accompany her. Confronting Cummings will however probably mean another dive in my already lowly standing in society if you are up to handling that.'

She smiled. 'I shall be right there beside you, Francis, and our reputations are the last thing to be worrying about. It's Anna we need to protect. But I remember something else Sally

Cummings told me. She said that she and her husband would be leaving for an extended tour of Italy at the end of the month and that they might not be coming back to England for a long time.'

'That's the effect of a stolen fortune in gold because, believe me, someone will know that he has it and will want a share too. It also means we have to move quickly though or otherwise he will be gone.

Sephora smiled. 'I used to be so scared of life I barely had an opinion, but now…'

'Now you are beside me identifying murderers and exposing them. I am not certain if that is such a good thing.'

She stopped him by bringing one finger to his lips.

'It is my salvation.'

Chapter Fourteen

They arrived in London late in the morning after seeing everyone safe at Montcliffe and letting Daniel and Amethyst Wylde know what it was that they were doing.

Anna clung on to them both as they left.

'When will you come back?'

'As soon as we have dealt with the man who tried to hurt you,' Francis stated. 'After that we can all live in complete safety.'

Maria was waiting for them with her maid in attendance at the Douglas town house as they arrived and she wanted to know every single thing that had happened since they had last been together. She also had surprising news of her own.

'Adam Stevenage has asked for my hand in marriage, but Papa is not pleased with the match and refuses to give his blessing. He thinks that if you did not marry a duke then I shall be able to. I am going to give him a month to get used to the idea and if he has not then I shall simply run away to Italy with Adam. It's a place I have always longed to go.'

Sephora watched Francis as he stood over by the window. Within a second of being in the house the problems of her family seemed to have landed upon him. But instead of being irritated as Richard would have been, he looked amused.

'Go to Venice and to Rome and then travel south to Naples to see Herculaneum and Pompeii.'

'You have been there?' Her sister looked astonished, but before he could answer the first question she had asked him another. 'You think I should go, then?'

'It sounds as if you have already made up your mind.'

'Mama and Papa and Josephine Allerly decry any place that is not England.'

'So our parents are talking with the Winburys again?' Sephora asked this because last she had heard they were not on speaking terms.

'Indeed they are. Josephine is at our house every second day because she is not happy with Richard's choice of bride-to-be and rues your loss.'

'His loss and my gain.' Francis came to stand next to Sephora and took her hand in his. Unexpectedly Maria blushed and began to mention the ball that was to be held the following evening.

'Richard and his newly betrothed will attend. Mama and Papa are going too.'

Sephora's heart sank at that information, but perhaps a ball might afford another opportunity.

'Are Richard's cousin Terence Cummings and his wife likely to be there?'

Maria laughed. 'I suppose if Richard is there then they will be too. I never liked him much and I thought Sally Cummings always seemed browbeaten. Perhaps being domineering and arrogant is a Winbury family trait? Why do you ask?'

'Cummings was there on the day Anna was snatched and I wanted to enquire if he saw anything we'd missed.' Not quite a lie, but not the truth either.

'You ought to be careful with him for I don't

trust him at all and Adam almost came to fisti-
cuffs with the man a week or so ago.'

'Why?' Francis asked this and Maria gri-
maced.

'He said something derogatory about you and
Adam took umbrage. Cummings actually tried
to get Adam to come into a business he'd invested in, something with liquor, I think, and he
said he was doing very well in it. Their heated
words put an end to that.'

When Maria was gone on the promise of seeing them tomorrow at the Clarkes' ball, Francis
pulled Sephora over to the window and brought
his arms about her. His embrace felt warm and
comforting.

'Everything that's said of Cummings draws
the noose tighter in about him. Daniel let me
know that he was seen in Hastings on the night
that Clive Sherborne died.'

'But it will be safe? You will be safe?'

'I will be and in public it might be easier to
get to him. He won't have the opportunity of refusal to see me, though with your parents in attendance I'll understand if you want to wait…'

'No.' Her answer was certain. 'I want this
finished with and Anna safe.'

He tipped her chin up and covered her lips with his own, a quiet languid kiss that turned suddenly into more. The quick streak of want made her breathless.

'If anything were to happen to you because of this…'

'It won't.'

Her finger drew a line down the edge of his cheek and settled on the scar. 'Amethyst said that you were decorated for bravery? Where are your medals?'

'In a drawer somewhere. There were a lot of other braver men who died doing the same thing as I did.'

'What was it you did to receive such an honour?'

He brought her closer so that she could feel the breath of him across her hair as he spoke.

'Our regiment was used to cover the movements of Moore's retreating army and to do that we were engaged in all the rearguard clashes. Between Lugos and Betanzos we lost more troops over a week than we did in the whole of the expedition altogether. It was the snow and the freezing rain—the mountain passes were slippery with ice and by that time discipline in the rank and file had broken down completely.'

'So it was every man for himself?'

'Well, it was and it wasn't. The French were close behind, you see, and the action at the back was causing as many deaths as the freezing temperatures further up. So I positioned myself on a hill overlooking the valley and picked the French off as I saw them, and little by little our troops got through.'

'And your cheek?'

'You can't stay unseen forever, or protected, as gunshot is easily traceable. A group of men came at me from behind and a sabre caught my face. If I hadn't turned when I did though it would have sliced off my head and I saved myself by falling down the ravine behind me, grabbing at rocks as I went to slow my descent.'

'Then you followed the others towards Corunna.'

'No. By then I'd lost a lot of blood and so I made for the closer port of Vigo. I travelled north-west at night mostly and found a ship home. The transports had left by the time I made it there, but a Spanish sea captain took pity on me and transported me to England. His wife fixed my face.'

'She sewed it up?'

'She couldn't do that because by then it was too inflamed. She poured hot water over the wound and made a poultice of bread and milk. Whatever paste she concocted to draw out the badness worked. The scar just reminds me of how lucky I was to survive.'

'But you don't value your medals?'

'War makes you realise heroism is a changing thing. One moment this and the next one that. I took my orders and did my duty like a hundred other officers in the continent and a lot of them died without recognition or praise.' He raised his hands up in front of him and looked down. 'Before that war I was a different man. I thought less about death and more of life.'

Sephora closed her own fingers about his. 'I was the same. When I fell into the water from that bridge there was a part of me that thought it might have been easier if it just ended then. But I've changed now...'

'...and we are both made whole.' He finished the sentiment for her.

Different words from the ones Richard had constantly bombarded her with. Not I love you, but much, much more. The truth had her reaching for him.

'Love me, Francis,' she said as he nuzzled into her throat.

'I will.'

She dressed carefully for the Clarkes' ball in a gown that she had always thought looked well upon her. It was made of heavy silk with a woven pattern of blue leaves in flossed satin around the bodice and hem. The light had a trick of catching the silk and satin in a way that made the fabric almost live. Teamed with long gloves and a velvet pelisse mirroring the shades of the dress she felt...braver. She smiled at the thought, but it was true.

If she was going into battle she needed to be looking her best. She'd not had one outbreak of hives since becoming Francis's wife.

Francis wore his usual black, stark and sombre, the cloth and cut of breeches and jacket a classical one. He'd queued his hair tonight in a way that was not as severe as he usually wore it, and it suited him. His one nod to the more decorative came in the wearing of his ruby ring. Sephora thought he had never looked more beautiful or more dangerous.

'If Cummings attacks, you need to leave immediately. Do you promise me this, Sephora? Should I have to worry about you, too, I will be distracted and if you were to be hurt…' He stopped and swallowed.

'What if Terence is armed?'

He lifted the left opening of his jacket and she saw the heft of a knife beneath and was glad for it.

'But could there be others with him, do you think? Others in the *ton*?'

'Anything is possible, I suppose, but I have a feeling he acts alone. Anna saw only him in the warehouse and you said he was leaving the country with his wife at the end of the month, so he is probably not the sort to want to share his spoils. Ralph Kennings was the same.'

'He was a loner?'

'He was a man who wanted to have it all and he did not care whom he trampled on to make it happen. I'd known him in the Continent before I left for the Americas.'

This was new. He'd never offered information like this unbidden before. She stayed quiet hoping he might say more.

'We were in Spain together. On the hills above the pass where I had dug in to try to help the soldiers from the regiment below and I saw Kennings turn and shoot a British officer. Later I found out it was his wife's brother he had killed and later still I discovered the woman herself had disappeared. Putting two and two together I think he got rid of them both because she was a wealthy heiress and he wanted the money. How wealthy is Sally Cummings?'

Sephora simply stared at him. 'Very. Her father protected her assets in a document that said she would not inherit anything until she had been married for ten years. He never liked Cummings, you see, but apart from limiting the access to her funds there was not much more he could do about it.'

'And how long has she been married now?'

'It must almost be that number. You think he would murder her?'

'Killing is easy after you have done it once.' The hard tone he used made Sephora frown. 'I barely blinked an eye when I shot Kennings. It was only afterwards that…'

He stopped.

'That you regretted it?'

'Yes.' This time the hazel in his eyes was glazed in pain and torment.

'I love you, Francis.' The words came without thought, and they came from her heart, body and soul. 'I have loved you from the first moment you gave me your breath beneath the water and every second since.'

Unexpectedly he laughed. 'I take you to my bed and love you in every way I have ever learnt with care and attention and fortitude and you do not say anything. Then when I confess that I have killed a murderer in cold blood and am sorry for it, you tell me this. Is there some law of logic that exists only in women, some way of tangling a man's thoughts until they do not have a mind of their own, until there is no certainty of anything any more? Save that of knowing I love you too.'

'You do?' She could barely utter the words with the thickness in her throat.

'When you fell off that bridge with your riding habit a living emerald in the sunshine and your tiny hat spiralling through the air behind, I thought...I thought if I could not find you beneath the water then I should die with the trying before I gave you up.'

Sephora smiled at such a truth. 'Was it pre-ordained do you think, a bee sting at that exact moment and a horse that would react so violent? One moment later and it would not have happened as it did or a moment sooner and you may have missed me altogether.'

'Love can be a powerful thing,' he whispered and reached for her hand. '*"Doubt truth to be a liar; But never doubt I love."* With me it will be always and forever, Sephora.'

She felt the tears pool in her eyes. 'When this is over I want you to take me home, Francis, and I want for us to have babies. Lots of them, as many as we can fill Colmeade House with for I am done with the *ton* and London town. All I need is you.'

The large ballroom at the Clarkes' town house was full and busy when they arrived and found their places with Gabriel and Adelaide Hughes, Daniel and Amethyst Wylde and Lucien, Alejandra and Christine Howard.

Sephora was glad Francis would not be alone in this quest and glad, too, that her parents were nowhere at all in sight. Despite the fighting words of a half an hour ago she felt nervous and worried though her elation with the proclamations that they had given each other also lingered.

She'd known she loved Francis for a long time and had felt the same regard back from him, but the words she had once censored were now valued and dear, no longer the oft repeated worthless and unimportant sentiments that they had been with Richard.

When a waltz struck up he leaned over and asked her to partner him. 'It will give us a better view of the room and those within it,' he said quietly as they took their place on the floor.

With his arms about her and the chandeliers above, Sephora simply leaned into his chest and felt, this moment, this second, with a husband who was good and strong and true. And beautiful, she added. So beautiful she could see a myriad women watching them, watching him. Her fingers tightened about his.

'Winbury is at the far end of the room, Sephora, but I can see no sign of Terence Cummings.'

She smiled, her musings so different from his alert watchfulness. Gabriel and Adelaide danced nearby and the Earl of Wesley's eyes scanned the room with the same purpose as Francis did.

Then Sally Cummings came into view, standing alone beside one of the large windows and looking upset. A sense of foreboding filled Sephora. How easily she could have been a woman exactly like her in ten years or so if she had married Richard, for the uncertain nervous expression was familiar; she had seen it so many times on her own face in the mirror.

When the waltz finished Francis led her from the floor towards her parents, who had now arrived and were standing on one side waiting for them.

'I hope you are well.' This greeting was given by her mother with some coldness though her father was a little more effusive.

'It is good to see you again, Sephora. I have missed you, but you look happy.'

'Is Maria here tonight?' She glanced around for her sister.

'Not yet. I think she will no doubt make an appearance a little later. Aunt Susan is with her.'

Her father turned then to Francis. 'I hope your ward is recovered after her fright in London, St Cartmail, and if there is anything I can do to help you find the culprits please do ask.'

'Thank you, Lord Aldford, but it is all in

hand and the man responsible for the kidnapping should soon be facing the law.' Francis was polite but distant and Sephora thought at this rate the two men should never know each other well enough to be friends. She was glad when Lucien Howard greeted Francis from behind and her parents moved on.

'Cummings is here. He was in the card room, but he has gone outside now for some air. He's been drinking heavily so you might want to be careful. I'll give you a few moments to sound him out.'

Thanking Lucien, Francis took her arm.

'I would ask you to go and stand with your parents, Sephora, but I can see it in your eyes that you will not go.'

Despite the situation his voice sounded relaxed, but then he had been in difficulties many times in his life before by all accounts and was probably well able to disguise any misgivings. Her own heartbeat pounded in her ears.

Francis scanned the space around them as they walked through the wide French doors. Two men at the far end of the terrace were engaged in conversation and at the other end a couple lingered.

Winbury's cousin was drinking, for two empty glasses sat on a marbled table near him and he held another one. A dash of anger crossed his face as they joined him.

'I did not think you were back in London, Lady Sephora. All my sources said that you were ensconced most happily at the Douglas family estate in the middle of Kent.'

'Indeed we were until this morning, but business has called us to the city.'

There was a look in Cummings's eyes that began to worry Francis and turning to Sephora he spoke quietly. 'Could you go inside and get me a drink? I find I am suddenly thirsty.'

He wanted his wife away from here and from undercurrents he could not quite understand for there was some wrongness in this situation that played about the edge of his caution. Sephora did not turn away though and as the two from further along the terrace moved closer he saw their faces for the first time. It was the men who had tried to take Anna in London though they were dressed far differently today. Cummings had known them after all, just as Sephora had said he did.

Pushing Sephora behind him he did not wait for them to attack. His first punch brought down the heavier man and he lay there motionless though the younger man had brought out a knife and was circling him with it.

Without hesitation Francis took his own blade from the strap at his breast and crouched, a flash of steel against the darkness as he moderated his breathing, slowing it down and steadying it before moving forward.

His opponent was good but Francis was better and within a few moments he was able to strike the weapon from the other's fist and bring his blade down into the soft flesh of the man's arm. He couldn't kill him, not here a few yards from a ball in progress and a room containing a hundred women who would be horrified by such violence.

Using the heavy handle he slammed down hard across the other man's head as the fellow ran at him and he too, fell to the floor.

Then things took an unexpected turn as Cummings lunged for Sephora and his grip was tight around her neck.

'Drop the knife, Douglas, or I will kill her.' The words were snarled and furious as Francis raised his hands. Sephora's face was deathly pale and her eyes were wide. As Cummings's fingers pressed deeper, Francis did exactly what he asked, laying the knife to one side of him and speaking quietly.

'It is over, Cummings. I know what you have done. You can only make it worse for yourself by harming an innocent.'

He moved sideways slowly as he spoke, the anger in him blood red and boiling. One second was all it would take to get to Cummings, but it had to be the right second. A neck could be broken easily with enough pressure and Sephora's was slender and small. He could do nothing at this moment but wait. The first man at his feet was recovering and he saw Cummings's eye flicker at the movement.

'Clive Sherborne was a colleague of yours, was he not?' Francis asked the question because in an impasse of this sort it was good to engage the participants in dialogue in order to buy time. He knew from experience that the longer these standoffs went on for the less likely someone would be hurt.

The man was arrogant enough to think he could still get away with murder, but Francis could see Lucien's outline against the doors.

'Clive Sherborne was an impediment. But why hurt Anna? What had the child done to harm you?'

'She was never a child, don't you see. She was his snitch, the one with the eyes and the brain. Without her that coward and thief would have never risen as he did through the ranks of the smugglers. Without her he'd have been dead long before he was.'

'My cousin saw you kill her father. She was hiding under the straw in the corner of the warehouse. She can identify you, Cummings, and she has.'

The older of the two men Francis had knocked down now sat up, a quiet movement that took Cummings's attention, and he loosened his grip.

It was enough.

Francis flung himself at Winbury's cousin knocking both him and Sephora over, coming up across Cummings quickly and punching him hard as his wife scrambled away. With his free foot he kicked the recovering miscreant in the head, pleased at the cracking sound of a skull hitting stone.

'Run, Sephora,' he ordered, wanting her out of the reach of any more violence, but instead she stayed where she was and spoke with feeling.

'You were there, Terence, there on the street when the man tried to kidnap Anna. I called to you for help, but you disappeared. You didn't want anyone to see you let alone a small girl who recognised you as the one who had murdered her father.'

'Prove it, Douglas.' Terence Cummings was so wrathful now he could barely get the words out, blood pouring down his face from a broken nose. 'Who'd believe you anyway, with your more-than-questionable reputation and the marks of a criminal around your throat?'

His shout drew others from the main ballroom out onto the terrace and Lucien came to stand beside him. Sally Cummings was there too, but she made no move to stand beside her husband, her face ashen and her eyes sunken.

Then Richard Allerly pushed through to kneel down to his bleeding cousin.

'If you have killed him, Douglas, I will have

you hanged properly this time and a good job, too, you bastard.'

The hushed anger of the gathering crowd was familiar and Francis tried to take in breath to answer, but his throat felt tight. Sephora's parents stood ten yards away behind him, the horror on their faces reflecting all that they imagined their daughter's life to have become.

A whole group of people who hated him and would not spare the time to even find out the truth. All of a sudden he could not even be bothered refuting the accusation. His eye ached, his hand and back, too, and one of the damned miscreants had managed to land a punch right on the wound of his healing shoulder.

A voice then rang out across all the others. It was Sephora and she was no longer anything like the girl he had first met. Now she was a furious avenging angel who faced the crowd with all the anger of the wrongfully damned and looked them all straight in the eyes.

These people thought the Earl of Douglas was the one at fault here, so easily and seamlessly, so without thought, explanation or reason. It was how the *ton* worked after all. Anyone who did not quite fit within its narrow confines was to be ostracised and excluded, cast out into the role of wrongdoer and disreputable.

Francis looked battered and defeated, the cut across his eyes sending blood onto his damaged cheek and he was holding his right-hand side and breathing harshly.

Well, she would fight every person on this terrace if necessary and then more besides to protect him. The anger pummelled through her like a living bolt of fire, untrammelled and vehement. He had been accused wrongly in the Hutton's Landing by a crowd baying for his blood and she would never let anything like that happen again here.

'Terence Cummings is the murderer… You all have it wrong. He was the one who killed Clive Sherborne and tried to kidnap a young child. He is a smuggler who makes money out of others' misfortunes and it was him who paid men to attack the Earl of Douglas on this terrace and in Kew Gardens. I swear this is true on the hope of my soul in Heaven.'

Lucien Howard and Gabriel Wesley had the men in hand and their presence added to her truths. Sally Cummings was crying profusely but in a softer tone now and she made no effort to refute the accusation.

'We'll take him to Bow Street.' Lucien said this and a murmur ran through the onlookers. She saw a quick communication go between him and Francis.

For so many years her husband had fought alone, managed alone, lived alone. Well, no longer. She would make certain he was seen by others in exactly the same way she saw him. Honourable and solid.

Without thought she faced the Duke of Winbury. 'Perhaps, Your Grace, you should be more careful about whom you associate with in the future. Your cousin appears to be everything you say he is not and we have the witnesses to prove it. He is a murderer, a kidnapper and a thief.' Her words were easily heard and she did not falter as she caught the face of her mother. Elizabeth looked shocked and pale. 'My husband and I will wait to receive your apology, Richard. I hope it will be forthcoming.'

With that she simply stepped back and threaded her arm through Francis' and without a backward glance they made their way from the terrace, through the colourful crowded ballroom, past the silent watchful musicians and out into the night. Hailing the waiting Douglas carriage, they quickly got in.

'It is over, Francis.' Sephora saw that he shook and the pallor of his skin was white.

'God' was his only reply and she laughed then, a way to relieve the tension she was to think later, a way to find a pathway through everything that had happened. He had given her breath beneath the bridge all those weeks ago and she was giving him some back right now. A space. A time to regather.

The small and utter truth of love.

This came without reflection or thought. It was the wholeness of them together, two halves that were perfectly melded and undeniably linked.

This was what marriage should be like. A formidable team who would fight everyone who tried to harm them and would be balanced and equal and honest. No one side dominant, no other side weakened. She would never let him down as certainly as she knew he would not disappoint her either.

'I love you, Francis,' she said and meant it. 'You are my heart.'

When he smiled back she placed her hand across his and watched as his bloodied and shaking fingers wound about her own.

Gabriel Hughes, Daniel Wylde and Lucien Howard came to the town house an hour and a half after they had arrived home and they were jubilant.

'Those who Cummings had employed to rough you up, Francis, were only too pleased to tell the truth of their part in the proceedings in order to escape heavier penalties. Sally Cummings herself provided the rest of the proof by promising to produce papers implicating her husband in the sale of illicit liquor across many outlets in the city. She said he needed to be locked up for good as he was a threat to each and every one of the upstanding citizens of London town.'

'Comprehensive, I'd say.' Francis was astonished. 'Why did she do it, do you think?'

'Oh, she told us that and in a voice that most of the *ton* would have been party to. She'd been bullied by him for far too long, she said. Her father had warned her of the nature of the man, but she had not listened. The Duke of Winbury looked nothing but furious at such aspersions towards his family.'

'Miss Julia Bingham made short shrift of the night I noticed.' Lucien Howard said this as he helped himself to a glass of Francis's best brandy. 'Your parents too, Sephora, were less than impressed by Winbury's defence of a man who was so patently lying. Your mother was crying, but this time I think it was at the realisation of her own foolishness in believing in the lies about your husband and the dispersing crowd itself felt much the same, Francis. I think you have been exonerated.'

'Out of great evil comes a goodness.' Gabriel Hughes muttered this and they all laughed, the relief of the evening's tension unfolding in a way they could never have truly predicted.

Sephora took her husband's hand in her own. If she ever lost him… She stopped herself. Once she had worried about things from dawn to dusk, but now with Francis at her side anything and everything was possible. She could breathe again, easily.

Chapter Fifteen

Two days later they were finally at Colmeade House and everything was back in place. Anna had been overjoyed at being home again and, after sitting down and reassuring her that all her worries were over, had easily settled to sleep that night.

'Mrs Billinghurst looked the prettiest I have ever seen her appear,' Sephora said softly as Francis and she lay in bed later that night, the curtains pulled back and the wide summer sky about them.

'Her husband died a long while ago and left her largely penniless. She is probably as relieved to have a home as Anna is. Timothy seemed well too, and Hopeful looks fatter than when we left him.'

'Mrs Wilson feeds him the best scraps from the kitchen. I've seen her do it. You are beset by a houseful of strays, Francis, who are all thriving here. Myself included.'

He laughed at that, the lines at the sides of his eyes creasing into humour. 'A houseful of family,' he amended, 'and I should never wish to change it.'

'What will happen to Terence Cummings do you think? And Sally?'

'Cummings will stand trial for the murder of Clive Sherborne and his wife will undoubtedly return to her family with a much better understanding of what she needs in a husband. She is still young and wealthy. Let's hope she chooses a man next time who is honourable.'

'My parents sent a note to ask if they might come down to visit when we are settled in again. It arrived today.'

'I'd like that.'

She sat up and looked at him directly. 'Would you? Even after all that has happened with them?'

'They were trying to protect you from difficulty and who is to say that I won't act the same when Anna brings home a suitor and he is not everything I'd hoped for her.'

'I wish I had known your parents and your sister. I wish they were here too, with us.'

'Perhaps they are. If I ever lost you, Sephora, I know that you would sit here right next to my heart. You would never be gone from inside me. I swear it.'

'You see that is why I love you, Francis. You do not parrot the words that mean nothing. You only ever give me a truth and after all the lies I am so thankful for it.'

'The truth?' His voice was hesitant, a tone in it so unlike the certainty she usually heard she felt a shift of worry. 'Can I tell you something, Sephora? Something that sounds…strange?'

He sat up now too, and leaned against the headboard, bringing her in beside him and tucking her there close.

'When you fell into the water I heard my sister's voice as clear as day, and as certain as I hear yours now beside me.'

'What did she say?'

'She said, *"Save her, Francis, and save yourself."* I heard her plainly and that has never happened to me before or since. And she was right.'

'Right?'

'We saved each other.'

She nodded. 'I've been writing poems in the book you gave to me. Can I read one to you?'

When he said he would like that she leaned over to the bedside table and opened the small top drawer, extracting her diary from it.

'It's not very good and you might think...'

He placed a finger over the words. 'Go on.'

Clearing her throat she began, though she felt as nervous as she had ever been before.

"You brought me from the darkness; And the cold of below; Up into the light of laughter and love; And breath that was mine to live in..."

'Breath,' he whispered when she had finished the next few verses and took her hand into his own. 'We gave each other breath, and what more from life could you want than that?'

'I love you, Francis, with all my heart.'

As his hands threaded through her hair he sealed her lips with his, pushing forward to find all that it was he offered.

He was her heart just as she was his. They had both been lost and were now found, the loneliness and uncertainty swept away in a wave of truth.

She had crossed a threshold and everything she had known was changed for finally she was home.

* * * * *

If you enjoyed this story, make sure you don't miss the first three books in Sophia James's THE PENNILESS LORDS *quartet*

MARRIAGE MADE IN MONEY
MARRIAGE MADE IN SHAME
MARRIAGE MADE IN REBELLION

And look for Christine's story
Coming soon

MILLS & BOON®

HISTORICAL

AWAKEN THE ROMANCE OF THE PAST

A sneak peek at next month's titles...

In stores from 16th June 2016:

- **The Unexpected Marriage of Gabriel Stone** – Louise Allen
- **The Outcast's Redemption** – Sarah Mallory
- **Claiming the Chaperon's Heart** – Anne Herries
- **Commanded by the French Duke** – Meriel Fuller
- **Unbuttoning the Innocent Miss** – Bronwyn Scott
- **The Innocent and the Outlaw** – Harper St. George

Available at WHSmith, Tesco, Asda, Eason, Amazon and Apple

Just can't wait?
Buy our books online a month before they hit the shops!
visit www.millsandboon.co.uk

These books are also available in eBook format!

Lynne Graham has sold 35 million books!

To settle a debt, she'll have to become his mistress...

Nikolai Drakos is determined to have his revenge against the man who destroyed his sister. So stealing his enemy's intended fiancé seems like the perfect solution! Until Nikolai discovers that woman is Ella Davies...

Read on for a tantalising excerpt from Lynne Graham's 100th book,

BOUGHT FOR THE GREEK'S REVENGE

'Mistress,' Nikolai slotted in cool as ice.

Shock had welded Ella's tongue to the roof of her mouth because he was sexually propositioning her and nothing could have prepared her for that. She wasn't drop-dead gorgeous... *he* was! Male heads didn't swivel when Ella walked down the street because she had neither the length of leg nor the curves usually deemed necessary to attract such attention. Why on earth could he be making *her* such an offer?

'But we don't even know each other,' she framed dazedly. 'You're a stranger...'

'If you live with me I won't be a stranger for long,' Nikolai pointed out with monumental calm. And the very sound of that inhuman calm and cool forced her to flip round and settle distraught eyes on his lean darkly handsome face.

'You can't be serious about this!'

'I assure you that I am deadly serious. Move in and I'll forget your family's debts.'

'But it's a *crazy* idea!' she gasped.

'It's not crazy to me,' Nikolai asserted. 'When I want anything, I go after it hard and fast.'

Her lashes dipped. Did he want her like that? Enough to track her down, buy up her father's debts, and try and buy rights to her and her body along with those debts? The very idea of that made her dizzy and plunged her brain into even greater turmoil. 'It's immoral… it's blackmail.'

'It's definitely *not* blackmail. I'm giving you the benefit of a choice you didn't have before I came through that door,' Nikolai Drakos fielded with a glittering cool. 'That choice is yours to make.'

'Like hell it is!' Ella fired back. 'It's a complete cheat of a supposed offer!'

Nikolai sent her a gleaming sideways glance. 'No the real cheat was you kissing me the way you did last year and then saying no and acting as if I had grossly insulted you,' he murmured with lethal quietness.

'You *did* insult me!' Ella flung back, her cheeks hot as fire while she wondered if her refusal that night had started off his whole chain reaction. What else could possibly be driving him?

Nikolai straightened lazily as he opened the door. 'If you take offence that easily, maybe it's just as well that the answer is no.'

Visit **www.millsandboon.co.uk/lynnegraham**
to order yours!

MILLS & BOON®

MILLS & BOON®

The One Summer Collection!

2 free books!

Join these heroines on a relaxing
holiday escape, where a summer fling
could turn in to so much more!

Order yours at **www.millsandboon.co.uk/onesummer**

MB523_OSA

MILLS & BOON®

Mills & Boon have been at the heart of romance since 1908... and while the fashions may have changed, one thing remains the same: from pulse-pounding passion to the gentlest caress, we're always known how to bring romance alive.

Now, we're delighted to present you with these irresistible illustrations, inspired by the vintage glamour of our covers. So indulge your wildest dreams and unleash your imagination as we present the most iconic Mills & Boon moments of the last century.

Visit **www.millsandboon.co.uk/ArtofRomance** to order yours!

0516_AOR